STO ✓ ✓

W9-BAZ-726

Kitty in the Summer

Books by Judy Delton:

Kitty in the Middle
Kitty in the Summer

Kitty
in the Summer

By JUDY DELTON

Illustrated by Charles Robinson

Houghton Mifflin Company   Boston   1980

ALLEN COUNTY PUBLIC LIBRARY
FORT WAYNE, INDIANA

Library of Congress Cataloging in Publication Data

Delton, Judy.
  Kitty in the summer.

  SUMMARY: Kitty's summer in the country is filled
with new experiences, from "purchasing" a pagan
baby to exposure to real poverty.
  [1. Minnesota — Fiction] I. Robinson, Charles,
1931-   II. Title.
PZ7.D388Kk   [Fic]   80-17665
ISBN 0-395-29456-8

Copyright © 1980 by Judy Delton

All rights reserved. No part of this work may be
reproduced or transmitted in any form by any means,
electronic or mechanical, including photocopying and
recording, or by any information storage or retrieval
system, without permission in writing from the publisher.

Printed in the United States of America

v 10 9 8 7 6 5 4 3 2 1

7015360

for Norine Odland

Contents

Kitty in the Summer

One

Vacation Begins

Kitty waved from the window of the train as it pulled out of the Union Depot in St. Paul. Her mother and father and Aunt Jo (who had driven them downtown) waved back. She watched them get smaller and smaller as the train gathered speed on its way to Norwood. The train was going west all the way to the Rocky Mountains, but Kitty would only ride the fifty miles to Aunt Katie's.

Kitty went to Norwood every summer. Aunt Katie was her father's sister, and she kept house for Kitty's grandfather and worked at the church two doors away, ringing the church bell for the Angelus, scraping wax off of the vigil-light holders, and ironing the priest's vestments. Kitty liked to help her, and she also looked forward to seeing Betsy, who was her age and lived next door to Aunt Katie.

Kitty rode the train because her father did not have a car. He always said, "Maybe when the war is over," but so far she and her mother and father took the streetcar or train or rode in Auntie Jo's 1939 Chevrolet when they had to go somewhere. Nineteen thirty-nine was the last year they had made cars before the war. Now, in 1942, Kitty knew, all the metal went into making weapons. Kitty bought war stamps every Tuesday at school to help build them. And with gas rationed, many people took the train now, even if they did have a car.

Kitty had a seat by the window. She liked that. It was cozy in the train, with her suitcase overhead on the rack and two candy bars to eat if she was hungry and her new book, *Wind's in the West,* on her lap. She didn't know if she should watch the scenery go by, or watch the people inside the train, or read her book. She decided to divide the time equally into thirds. It took almost three hours to get to Norwood. That would be one hour to watch people, one to watch scenery, and one to read— that is, if she didn't go to the dining car. If she went to the diner, she would have to concentrate on ordering her food and making sure her milk didn't spill and not talking to strangers and worrying about how much to leave the waiter for a tip.

"Minneapolis!" called the conductor as he came through the train, punching tickets. "Minneapolis!" The only people who took the short train trip to Minneapolis from St. Paul were schoolchildren who had never ridden on a train before. Kitty's father had taken her to Minneapolis on the train when she was five. They had had lunch and bought a souvenir (Kitty still had it: a mother-of-pearl penknife that had "Souvenir of Minneapolis" and a picture of Minnehaha Falls printed on it), and then they had taken a Greyhound bus back home. Kitty smiled, remembering how young she had been. Now she was almost in fifth grade. She straightened her cotton dress over her knees. Her mother had put so much starch in it that instead of lying flat, it stood out stiffly all around her.

The train rolled to a stop in the Minneapolis depot. It is sure faster to get to Minneapolis on the train than on the streetcar, thought Kitty. It seemed as though they had just left St. Paul. Kitty watched the people walk down the narrow aisle with their suitcases and bags. Most of them were servicemen with duffel bags over their shoulders. There were sailors in white bell-bottomed trousers and round white hats over their foreheads or on the back of their heads. There were soldiers in khaki and Marines in green. Outside the window, mothers and fathers and wives were hugging more servicemen and crying and waving goodbye. "Be sure to write," they called. Kitty knew some servicemen. Her cousin Don sent her V-Mail letters from Guam, and her Uncle Joe was in a foxhole in Italy.

"Is this seat taken?" asked a breathless woman in a flowered seersucker dress and with an umbrella and a knitting bag in her hand.

"No," said Kitty. "It isn't."

The woman smiled and put her umbrella up on the rack and then sat down beside Kitty. "I'm Mrs. Iverson, and I'm going to Marshall," she said, offering her hand.

Kitty shook it and gave her name and explained where she was going. "I have an uncle in Marshall," said Kitty. "John Rictor."

"Why," said Mrs. Iverson, "he is the postmaster!"

Kitty nodded.

"What a small world!" Mrs. Iverson said.

Kitty never understood what people meant when they said the world was small. After all, the world was one size and it didn't change as far as she knew. If the world was anything at all, it was big, with all those countries in her geography book that she had never heard of before and places on maps where she would never go. This woman should know how big the world is, thought Kitty. But other people said "It's a small world," too, so perhaps they knew something she didn't.

"I was visiting my sister in Minneapolis, but it's good to be going back home," Mrs. Iverson chattered. "Minneapolis is nice to visit, but I wouldn't want to live there." She laughed.

Kitty wondered what was the matter with living in Minneapolis, but she didn't ask. As far as she knew, it was a fine place to live, with all the lakes to swim in during the summer.

"It's always good to get home," went on Mrs. Iverson, taking her knitting out of the bag.

Kitty thought it was far more fun to go away than to come home, but she nodded. Good heavens, there wasn't anything this woman said that she agreed with!

"Do you knit?" said Mrs. Iverson.

"No, but my friend Margaret Mary does," said Kitty. "Margaret Mary knit six pairs of mittens for the Red Cross last winter, all by herself."

Mrs. Iverson looked at Kitty. "My . . ." she said, "what a fine thing."

"Margaret Mary can do everything," said Kitty. "She can bake bread and can peaches and embroider pillowcases. And she gets all A's in school," Kitty added.

"Why, she sounds very talented," said Mrs. Iverson.

"Oh, she is," said Kitty. "She knows all the mysteries of the rosary and she's the best artist at St. Anthony's. She could probably sell her paintings."

Kitty stopped to think. Margaret Mary probably couldn't sell her paintings. Kitty must be exaggerating again. She always exaggerated. She started to tell a story and before long she couldn't remember if what she was saying was real or make-believe. When she went to confession, it was hard to know whether or not to say she lied. She decided exaggeration must be only about half as bad as a real lie, so she counted two exaggerations as one lie.

"Well, maybe she couldn't *sell* them," said

Kitty, catching herself and saving a half-lie from having to be confessed. "But she is a good artist."

Mrs. Iverson kept knitting and asking Kitty questions, and as the conductor called out, "Glencoe . . . Chaska . . . Young America," Kitty told Mrs. Iverson about her two best friends, Margaret Mary and Eileen. Eileen was more daring than Margaret Mary. She was an only child like Kitty, and had bouncing yellow curls and took tap-dancing lessons. With Eileen Kitty played grown-up games, like confession and dress-up, and with Margaret Mary she played paper dolls. Kitty told Mrs. Iverson about the fun the three of them had together at St. Anthony's School in St. Paul.

Mrs. Iverson seemed to enjoy the stories, so after Kitty told her about Margaret Mary and Eileen, she told her about Aunt Katie in Norwood and how she always went to Norwood every summer and how Margaret Mary stayed home and helped her mother. Just as Kitty began to tell Mrs. Iverson about her actress friend, Miss Neilson, the conductor came through and called, "Norwood! Next stop Norrrrwood!"

Kitty couldn't believe it. She had planned the three hours so carefully. Now she was in Norwood and she hadn't looked at the scenery or watched the people—other than Mrs. Iverson—or read her book.

She jumped to her feet as the train slowed down and steamed to a stop. A tall blond sailor reached for her suitcase, and Mrs. Iverson hugged her and said, "I'll say hello to your uncle Johnny tomorrow morning in the post office!"

Kitty was the only one getting off at Norwood. The porter put a little metal stool down on the ground and helped her down the steps, all the while brushing her with his whiskbroom and handing her her suitcase. As Kitty gave him a quarter she thought, "Good heavens, I could have missed my stop and ridden all the way to the Rocky Mountains." She wondered briefly what would have happened if she had, and felt afraid. She would have had to call her mother and father and they would have wired her money and been upset that she was alone in a strange place. Her father might even have had to leave work to come and get her. Kitty shuddered. She would have to pay more attention to what she was doing.

Kitty saw Aunt Katie waiting just where she always did, by the side of the wooden depot, with her two hands clutching her handbag and her brown and gray hair pulled back from her face and swept into a pug at the back of her head. Kitty ran along the platform toward Aunt Katie as the train pulled away. "I almost rode on to Marshall!" said Kitty.

"*Gott in Himmel!*" said Aunt Katie. "What would I have told your father?"

Kitty laughed. Aunt Katie often said part of her sentences in German. Norwood was a German town. It had two churches, the German Lutheran where Betsy went and the German Catholic where Aunt Katie and Grandpa went. Kitty didn't understand German because no one she knew in St. Paul spoke German, but that didn't matter, because everyone in Norwood that Kitty knew usually spoke English. Even her grandpa, who had come from Germany when he was twenty-one, spoke some English.

Kitty and Aunt Katie crossed the railroad tracks and started walking home. On the way, Kitty told her about Mrs. Iverson and Margaret Mary and Eileen. Aunt Katie told Kitty about how the garden needed rain and that any time now she would be going out to the country to take care of a family while the mother had a new baby. Aunt Katie often helped families when someone was married or died or was born.

Before long they turned into a gravel alley and Kitty could see Aunt Katie's garden. The garden took up a whole town lot and every vegetable that anyone would want to eat grew in it. Every kind of flower grew there as well. In the fall Aunt Katie dug potatoes and stored them with carrots and other vegetables in the cold, damp cellar with a dirt floor under the house. She made pickles from the cucumbers and preserved the corn and peas and berries in heavy glass jars. Aunt Katie even canned her own meat. When a relative in the country butchered, Aunt Katie canned veal in glass jars, and all winter long she and Grandpa ate what was stored in the cellar. In St. Paul, people had victory gardens, but none was as big as Aunt Katie's regular garden, which she had whether there was a war or not.

"There's Grandpa!" shouted Kitty as she set her suitcase down in the alley and ran to greet him. Aunt Katie picked up the suitcase and followed.

"Hello, Grandpa!" said Kitty, holding out her hand to shake his, because her grandpa wasn't the kind of person you hugged.

"*Wie geht's, wie geht's,*" he said from behind his gray mustache. He patted Kitty's head as though he wasn't quite sure who she was, even though she came every summer and during the winter Kitty's father mailed him Kitty's

report cards from St. Anthony's. Besides being an only child, Kitty was an only grandchild, and she couldn't understand how her grandpa could forget her. Her mother said Grandpa was old, and Aunt Katie always said he was doing poorly and his mind was failing, so perhaps that was it. Either that or he just plain didn't like her.

Grandpa wore his farm overalls, even though he had not farmed in years, and his felt bedroom slippers with the Indian on them, and he had his pipe in his mouth. He was standing on the steps as though he had been waiting for them. When Aunt Katie came closer, he took a watch out of his pocket and looked at it.

"Almost dinner time, Pa," Aunt Katie said in German, very loudly, because Grandpa was a little deaf. "You go upstairs, Kitty, take your grip upstairs. I'm going to ring the church bell, then we'll have dinner."

Aunt Katie dashed out the door and down the alley to the church, which was just on the other side of Betsy's house. Kitty went in the house, and as soon as she opened the door she knew she was in Norwood. The wood stove was going, and the air smelled like a mixture of burning wood and kerosene and Aunt Katie's sugar cookies and geraniums. The plants stood on the windowsills in their clay pots with china saucers underneath. Kitty walked over to one of them and rubbed the green fuzzy leaf between her fingers. She did that with tomato leaves in the garden, too; it was such a nice smell to have on your fingers. Grandpa sat in his wooden rocker that squeaked and smoked his pipe and seemed to look over the top of Kitty's head instead of at her.

She picked up her suitcase and ran through the kitchen and dining room and up the stairs to the big bedroom she shared with Aunt Katie. It had two double iron beds with feather mattresses and down pillows and homemade quilts on them. Kitty stood in the doorway and smelled how different the room was from hers at home. She never knew what it was, but it made her feel safe and cozy and reminded her of fresh air and clean clothes on a line. It was a little bit like mothballs and the blessed palm that was woven into wreaths and ropes and crosses and was entwined behind pictures of the Blessed Virgin Mary and behind statues of the Sacred Heart. There were geraniums on the windowsill, and Kitty smelled those, too. The quilt frame was standing up in the hall with a quilt on it, as though Aunt Katie had been working on it recently, and over in the middle of the room was the big hole in the floor for a stovepipe. Kitty loved to look down at the people walking below in the kitchen. In the morning, warm air and warm smells drifted up from the iron range below.

Kitty pulled out the drawers of the bird's-eye maple dresser with the carving of scrolls and cupids along the edge. The drawers were lined with newspaper, and Kitty took her clothes out of her suitcase and arranged them all in two of the drawers. She put her suitcase behind the curtain in the hall. Then she hung up her dresses and walked around upstairs into the other rooms, enjoying the feeling of being in Norwood again.

The storeroom door had a latch that fell into a slot instead of a doorknob. Kitty lifted it now and went in. It smelled faintly of spices and cedar. In the corner was a wicker doll buggy that Kitty had played with when she was small, and boxes and boxes of old pictures— pictures of stately old-fashioned ladies on their wedding day, with their hands on their husbands' shoulders. The husbands sat in chairs, and the wives stood. Aunt Katie had told Kitty they were all "old dead relatives" and had waved her hand as if to say they were not of any importance now that they were dead. Kitty glanced at them and wondered if people mattered after they were dead. Surely no one seemed to care about all the people in these boxes, who must have had a life something like Kitty's once, long ago. She wondered if all those pictures her mother and father took of her with her dolls on the front lawn and with Margaret Mary and Eileen squinting into the sun would end up in someone's attic some day, squashed flat in boxes belonging to strangers. It made her nervous to think of that, and she went out and latched the door and started downstairs.

Aunt Katie was back and busy in the kitchen, mixing strawberries with sugar in a bowl for shortcake. "Berries from the garden already," she said, "and wilted lettuce. Been some warm days already, ain't so." Aunt Katie said "ain't so" after many of her sentences, not so much as a question as a definite statement. "Ain't so" meant she was right, and no one ever thought of disagreeing. Kitty nodded her head. Aunt Katie poured vinegar and cream and crumbled bacon over the lettuce. Then she sliced the roast beef. The white damask tablecloth was on the dining-room table, and Kitty set the three plates around, and the familiar silverware that didn't match, from the kitchen pantry.

"Komm essen, komm essen!" called Aunt Katie loudly, so that Grandpa as well as Kitty could hear. He was dozing in his rocker. *Komm*

essen meant "come and eat" in German, and Aunt Katie was putting the food on the table and waving Grandpa to come and sit down.

At home Kitty had a sandwich for lunch, but in Norwood everyone had a big dinner at noon, even on Monday. Kitty was hungrier than she thought after her train ride, and it felt good to sit down at the dinner table.

"Kitty, will you say grace?" said Aunt Katie.

The three of them made the sign of the cross, and Kitty said, all in one breath, "Bless us O Lord and these thy gifts which we are about to receive from thy bounty through Jesus Christ our Lord Amen."

Grandpa slid his peas onto his knife and poured his coffee into his saucer to cool.

"After dinner," said Aunt Katie between bites, "Kitty and I will pick some gooseberries in the woods for a pie for supper."

Grandpa nodded and muttered *ja* and soaked his bread in Aunt Katie's gravy. Kitty tried hard not to spill food on her clean starched dress. Her summer in Norwood had begun.

Two

Money for a Puppy

Kitty and Aunt Katie picked gooseberries and made many pies that week. They went to church and cleaned the sacristy and scraped wax from the vigil lights. Aunt Katie played the organ and sang for the funeral Masses, and Kitty sat on the organ bench with her and turned the pages of the music. They got up early every morning to ring the church bell and fell into their featherbeds, tired out, at the end of the day. On Wednesday evening they went to the movie downtown because that was the night the theater gave dinnerware away with tickets. Aunt Katie was collecting the dishes with the pink roses and the scalloped gilt edges.

But the event that took most of Aunt Katie's time was the church bazaar. The women in the parish were planning the dinner they would cook and met often to discuss who would bake the pies and which farmer would donate a pig or a cow to butcher for the main dish. The dinner was always held in the church basement, while the bingo games and other raffles were held under a big canvas awning in the large side yard of the church. Kitty loved to play bingo, but something even more exciting was happening at the bazaar this year. Father Wallace was raffling off a black Labrador puppy. The puppy was kept in the back of the rectory in a wire pen, and Kitty stopped to talk to him every time she went there with Aunt Katie to visit the housekeeper, Emily.

"That's a fine dog," Emily said. "Purebred Lab. Be a good hunter."

"*Ach*—the *hund*," said Aunt Katie. *Hund* meant "dog" in German, but always sounded like "hound" to Kitty. Kitty wasn't thinking of hunting. She was thinking of how she had always wanted a dog more than anything in her whole life. But her mother would never buy one. She said she'd never have a dog in her house, tracking up the kitchen floor and leaving hair all over, but Kitty thought that since she was an only child with no prospects of a brother or sister, her mother's attitude was unfair. Besides, if she won a dog, it wouldn't be her fault. How could she help it if she just happened to take a chance and her ticket was drawn? All Kitty had to do was be absolutely sure her ticket *was* drawn. She could picture it now: her own live puppy in the back seat of Auntie Jo's car, riding home. She would teach him to play dead and roll over and sit up and beg and heel, and she'd take him for walks and save her allowance for rubber bones.

"I'd love to have that dog," she said to Aunt Katie. "I really want him."

"*Ach,*" said Aunt Katie, "What do you want a dog for?"

"He'd be a friend," said Kitty. "I've never had a pet of my own."

"*Ach*," said Aunt Katie again, as if she hadn't heard her, "What do you want a dog for?"

Every time Kitty saw the puppy and patted him, she knew she had to own him. He began to recognize Kitty and wag his tail when he saw her coming. Kitty called him Damien because Father Wallace said he was born on the feast day of St. Cosmas and Damien, and Cosmas sounded like a flower.

"I just have to win him," she said to Betsy one morning as they were sitting on the church steps in the sun, eating raw rhubarb. Betsy was German Lutheran, but she knew as much about the Catholic Church as she did about her own. When Kitty came in the summer, the two girls spent a good part of the day playing Mass on Aunt Katie's chicken coop. They spread an old lace tablecloth over the coop, and Betsy brought a bouquet of lilacs from her yard to put on top. Kitty was always the priest. When she said "*Dominus vobiscum*" Betsy said, "*Et*

23

cum spiritu tuo." She knew many Latin words and how to genuflect and strike her breast at the Confiteor.

"I s'pose the more chances you buy, the better chance you have to win," said Betsy.

Kitty thought about that. "Yes, one wouldn't be enough. I'd like to buy lots of chances. Maybe even all of them," she added.

"I don't think they'd let you buy them all, but maybe half," said Betsy. *"All* wouldn't be fair. It would be like buying a dog."

"I couldn't buy a dog," said Kitty thoughtfully. "My mother would never let me buy one. But if I won one, it would be like it wasn't even my fault."

"How much money do you have?" said Betsy, being practical.

"Not much," said Kitty. "About a quarter. That would only be five chances. And then I couldn't play bingo."

The girls thought some more. "You have to get more money," said Betsy. "A lot more."

"How?" asked Kitty. "How do people get money around here?"

"They either get a job or gamble," said Betsy. "My uncle gambles."

Kitty looked up. "I couldn't get a job," she said. "I'm not old enough to be a waitress, and anyway Aunt Katie wouldn't let me do that."

"Well, you couldn't gamble," said Betsy. "Gambling is against your religion. And you're not old enough, anyway."

"Aunt Katie hates gambling," said Kitty soberly.

"My dad says bingo is gambling," said Betsy.

"That's different," said Kitty. "It's for charity. If it's for the church, it's not gambling."

Betsy looked doubtful.

"Well, Aunt Katie wouldn't do it if it was wrong," she said. "Or Father Wallace, for Pete's sake."

"I know how you could get some money for the bazaar!" said Betsy, standing up suddenly. "Slot machines! They have slot machines in the drugstore and in the shoe store and two in the butcher shop!"

Kitty snapped her fingers. "That's it!" she said. "I played the slot machines up at the lake when we went on vacation. But I didn't win anything," she said, sitting down. "You don't always win."

"It still seems like the best way to get money."

"I think it's the only way," said Kitty. "I wonder if it's a sin to gamble?" She tried to run the church commandments through her mind.

"It's not a sin for me. I could gamble for you," offered Betsy generously.

There were surely advantages in having a Protestant friend, thought Kitty. "Let's go!" she said.

Kitty ran into the house and upstairs to get her quarter from the dresser drawer that had her clothes in it. "Aunt Katie?" she called.

Grandpa was smoking his pipe and reading

The Wanderer, a church newspaper written in German. Kitty wondered how anybody could understand those meaningless words. She looked out on the porch and in the garden. She didn't see Aunt Katie anywhere.

"I'm going uptown, Grandpa," called Kitty. "UPTOWN!" she called in a louder voice. "Tell Aunt Katie I'll be back in a little while."

Grandpa looked away from his paper and over her head. He didn't say anything. Kitty waved and ran out the door.

Kitty and Betsy ran all the way down the hill and across the tracks and up past the depot to the drugstore.

"You need nickels," said Betsy. "The slot machine takes nickels."

"The druggist will give me change," said Kitty.

"Sure enough," said the druggist when Kitty asked. "Five, ten, fifteen, twenty, twenty-five."

"Thank you," said Kitty, and the two girls walked over to the corner. Betsy rattled the slot machine.

"It feels full," she whispered. "Give me your nickel."

Kitty shivered. "Star light, star bright, first star I see tonight, I wish I may, I wish I might have this wish I wish tonight."

Betsy looked at her. "It isn't night," she said. "That only works when there are stars out."

Kitty crossed her fingers. Betsy put the nickel in and pulled the metal lever on the side. Pictures of oranges and apples and lemons and perfect little cherries spun around. For Kitty to win, three of the same kind had to appear in a row when the spinning stopped. The girls watched. The first to stop was a plum. Kitty closed her eyes. When she opened them, there was a lemon. And the third was an orange.

"Not even close," said Betsy in disgust. "Let's try again."

"We can't spend all the nickels," said Kitty in a panic. "At least not on one machine that is a loser."

"Let's go to the shoe store," said Betsy.

Kitty put her four remaining nickels in her pocket, and they ran down the street to the shoe store. The slot machine was standing right inside the door. Kitty handed Betsy a nickel, then closed her eyes and listened while Betsy pulled the handle. She listened to the spinning noise it made. Clunk, clunk, clunk, it went as the machine came to a stop. Kitty opened her eyes. Two plums and a bunch of cherries.

"Darn!" said Betsy, stamping her foot.

"Ah, that's close," said the shopkeeper, who was looking on. "But close only counts in horseshoes." He laughed.

Kitty felt like crying. She had three nickels left; they were going fast. Maybe she should use them for three chances on Damien.

"No," said Betsy. "The butcher shop is better. Let's go there."

Kitty was doubtful, but she followed Betsy down the street and turned in at the door of the meat market.

"I can only spend two more," whispered

Kitty. "Otherwise I won't have any money for the collection in church, or even one bingo game."

"Don't worry," said Betsy confidently. "You'll have lots of money. Just wait."

"Two pounds of Polish sausage, Joe," said a man in front of the slot machines. The man put a nickel in one of the machines. Then he put a nickel in the other. "One-armed bandits," he said to the girls, smiling. He put two more nickels in. Nothing happened. "Two more and that's it," he said. The machines spun the colored fruit around. Orange, lemon, plum. The other showed lemon, lemon, cherries.

"Hey Joe, don't these things ever pay off?" said the man.

Joe handed him the package of Polish sausage tied up in white paper. "Sure, sure, you just got to put that magic coin in," Joe said, laughing.

The man left, and Kitty and Betsy slipped up to the machines.

"These are bad luck," said Kitty. "That man put in six nickels and didn't win a thing."

"All the better," said Betsy. "There'll be more money in the machine for you." She was enjoying playing the slot machines with Kitty's money.

"Now, just these two nickels," said Kitty.

"I think we should put both nickels in one machine," said Betsy. "It increases the odds, I heard my uncle say that."

Betsy's uncle would probably know, Kitty thought. She crossed her fingers for luck. "This one," said Kitty, pointing to a machine.

Betsy put the nickel in. Kitty made the sign of the cross. Around spun the pictures.

"Cherries, cherries, and . . . *darn!*" said Betsy. "An orange!"

She put the last nickel in and pulled the lever. Kitty made the sign of the cross again.

"Ssshhh," said Betsy.

Kitty closed her eyes tightly. All of a sudden she heard a tremendous noise. After the clunk, clunk, clunk, there was a loud clatter, and

Kitty opened her eyes to see nickels pouring out of the machine—more nickels than she had ever seen in her life! They poured onto the floor, over her shoes, and down into her anklets. Betsy was screaming and had her arms cupped as if to catch them, but they poured over her arms and onto her feet as well.

"I don't believe it!" said Kitty. "I don't believe it!"

"I told you!" said Betsy. "I told you you'd win!" Betsy was jumping up and down on top of the nickels.

"Lawsy, you did hit the jackpot!" said the owner of the butcher shop, coming over with a brown paper bag. "Just look at that! Hasn't paid off for a month, this machine. You had the right nickel, girlie." He helped Kitty and Betsy round up all the slippery silver nickels and put them in a bag. "Hey, we need another bag," he said to the small crowd that had gathered around the machine.

"Which machine was it?" asked a woman nearby.

Betsy showed her. "Three oranges in a row," she said proudly.

"Well, I'll have to try that machine," said the woman. "I never have any luck at the drugstore."

The butcher helped the girls fill two bags with the nickels, and the girls started to leave.

"Boy, are these heavy," said Betsy. "You must be a millionaire, Kitty! I can hardly lift them."

As Kitty turned around, she heard a familiar voice. "Clara is bringing two mince," the voice said. "You're bringing the pig's knuckles, ain't so."

Betsy heard the voice at the same time. "Don't turn around," she whispered nervously, "but do you know who just came in here?"

"Aunt Katie," said Kitty. "What will we do?"

"She's by the door," said Betsy. "She's probably going to buy some meat."

Kitty nodded. "She gets summer sausage here," she said. "Is there a back door?"

Betsy shook her head.

"She's coming over to the counter—she'll see us!" whispered Kitty.

"Come on," said Betsy. "Back here."

Kitty followed her behind a life-sized cardboard figure of Uncle Sam that was standing in a corner near the slot machines. It said: UNCLE SAM WANTS YOU. Kitty never liked the look Uncle Sam had in his eye as he pointed his cardboard finger at her. If she were a man, she would never enlist in the Army, simply because of that look in his eye. Of course, it wasn't really Uncle Sam—perhaps the real Uncle Sam *was* friendly.

"Your aunt can't see us back here!" whispered Betsy.

"And Kathryn, what can I do for you today?" said the butcher, slapping his palm down on top of the meat case.

The girls shivered behind Uncle Sam.

"A pound of your summer sausage, nice and lean," said Aunt Katie.

"Just made it yesterday," said the butcher.

"Nice and fresh, nice and lean." He whistled as he wrapped the sausage. "Some good growing weather we've been having," he added.

"Pretty dry; we could use some rain, ain't so."

"*Ja ja,* we could use some of that, Kathryn."

"She's leaving," said Betsy, looking out from behind Uncle Sam. "And the butcher is in the cooler. Let's run for it!"

The girls gathered the brown bags full of nickels, and as soon as they saw Aunt Katie start toward the post office, they ran toward the depot. Just as they crossed the train tracks and started up the hill, the bag of nickels that Kitty was carrying broke.

Betsy hit her forehead with the heel of her hand. "*Gott!*" she said in German. "We'll never get them all!"

They watched the nickels rolling down the sidewalk and into the grass.

"We have to get them—every one! I need them to win Damien," said Kitty.

The girls got down on the sidewalk and

scrambled after all the nickels. When they had gathered them into a pile, Kitty sat down on the curb and took off her shoes. Then she took off her anklets. She held them up. "Put the nickels in here," she said. Kitty's mother always darned her socks neatly, and they never had holes. The girls filled both socks with nickels and put the rest in Kitty's shoes.

"We could have exchanged all these nickels for dollar bills at the bank!" said Betsy.

"Oh, no," said Kitty. "We'd probably meet Aunt Katie in the bank, and anyway, it looks like a lot more in nickels."

"I think it's more in paper money, or silver dollars," said Betsy, getting up with the heavy paper bag.

As they turned into the alley, Kitty said, "Let's go in the shed and count it; no one will see us there."

The girls opened the door of the shed where Grandpa's Model A Ford had been resting on four wooden blocks since he became too old to drive it.

"Wow!" said Betsy, as they dumped the money in a pile. "Just look at that! You could buy ten dogs!"

They put the nickels in small piles of one dollar each. When they were through, they counted the piles.

"Thirteen dollars!" said Kitty.

"No wonder they were so heavy," said Betsy. "You could buy 260 ice-cream bars," she added, full of respect for Kitty's new status.

Kitty picked up three of the piles. "These are for you, Betsy."

"No, they're yours," said Betsy quickly.

"You won them for me. You should get at least three dollars for doing that."

Betsy thought about it. "Well, if you're sure . . ." she said.

"That leaves me ten dollars. Ten dollars' worth of chances on Damien!" said Kitty. "I know I'll win him, Betsy, I just know I'll win him."

Betsy waved goodbye, and Kitty went up to the bedroom, where she put her two anklets full of nickels in the drawer under her underwear. Aunt Katie was just calling *"Komm essen"* as she started down to dinner, barefoot.

Three

Kitty Buys a Baby

As the bazaar grew closer, workmen appeared on the church lawn, nailing up booths and setting up tables and benches for bingo in a large square with an awning over them. Kitty and Betsy went over and watched them right after breakfast every day.

"That's it!" said Kitty one morning. "That's the pen for Damien!" They watched as the men put poles in the ground and strung chicken wire around them to make an enclosure for the puppy. Later that day the men hung a bright sign on the pen that read: WIN THIS PUREBRED LABRADOR HUNTING DOG."

"I will!" Kitty said emphatically to Betsy.

"I have to win that dog. I'll never have another chance." She went to the back of the rectory and talked to Damien. "Don't worry, boy, you'll be all mine tomorrow."

At supper that evening, Kitty said to Aunt Katie and Grandpa, "I'm going to win the dog tomorrow at the bazaar. I just have to win him."

Grandpa slid his potatoes onto his knife with a piece of homemade bread dipped in gravy, and swallowed the coffee from his saucer.

"He knows me, you know," said Kitty. "I mean, it's just like he's my dog already. He starts to bark and jump up and wag his tail when he sees me coming."

"*Ach,* you don't want a dog," said Aunt Katie, as though this was something new that Kitty was saying and she had never heard before that Kitty wanted a dog.

Kitty stared at her. Aunt Katie sometimes had a way of not knowing what someone had just said or done—like when Kitty had eaten three pieces of her apple pie and Aunt Katie said, "Here, have some pie—eat something," just as though she hadn't noticed that Kitty *had* been eating—for an *hour*.

"I do want a dog," said Kitty. "I want that dog. And I'm going to win him tomorrow."

"*Ach,* you don't want a dog," said Aunt Katie again, standing up and clearing the table. She pumped water into the teakettle and set it on the iron range to heat for washing dishes. Grandpa was still eating, and as soon as he finished Kitty cleared the rest of the things from the table. Grandpa sat in his rocker and lit his pipe and picked up *The Wanderer*.

"We'll go over and set up tables in the basement for the dinner when we finish here," said Aunt Katie, her hands in the pan of dishwater on the kitchen table.

When the dishes were put away, Aunt Katie hung the dish towel over the clothesline, and they started down the gravel alley to church. Some of the parishioners were pounding a horseshoe stake in the ground, and women were putting out the bingo prizes under the awning of the stand. Betsy was coming up the hill from town, eating an ice-cream bar that was melting down her arm.

"I'll help," she said, when she heard where Kitty was going. They passed the pen, fresh and new and waiting until morning for Damien. Then they went through the narrow doorway and down the worn stone steps to the cool dampness of the church basement.

"You put the tables in rows—here, like so. I'll get the dishes from the cupboards."

Kitty and Betsy arranged the long tables in neat rows and spread them with white starched tablecloths that the ladies of the parish had supplied. Then they took the cracked and chipped dishes that Aunt Katie brought from the church kitchen and set them around on the tables with the mismatched silverware and cups and saucers.

"I like church when no one is around," said Kitty. "It's so big and quiet."

"Let's play the organ," said Betsy, running up to the old pump organ in a corner of the basement. It had been put there when the church got a new pipe organ, and it was old and dusty. Betsy sat on the carpet-covered organ stool. She pumped away at the pedals and flipped the ivory stops open and swept her hands up and down the keyboards as if she were playing a real song. Then she sang "Here Comes the Bride" as she played a tuneless melody. Kitty swept down an imaginary aisle, bringing one foot up behind the other slowly as she had seen brides do. She held an imaginary bouquet of red roses in her arms.

"*Ach,*" said Aunt Katie, putting salt and pepper shakers on the tables. "You'll wake the dead," she called. "Come and put up the streamers and balloons."

The girls forgot about the organ and weddings and ran to blow up balloons and pull the edge of the crepe paper to make ruffles. The rest of the afternoon they hung the paper in big swooping loops from one corner of the basement to the other. In the middle, over the tables, hung the balloons they had blown up.

"Tomorrow we'll put flowers on the tables," said Aunt Katie.

"Tomorrow I'll be the owner of a dog!" said Kitty.

"*Ach,*" said Aunt Katie, "You don't want a dog."

On the way home, Betsy and Kitty gave one last pat to Damien, who was wagging his tail. He was so happy to see them he put two feet in his food dish.

The next morning Aunt Katie was up early, baking pies before Mass. Sweet warm berry smells came up through the hole in the floor when Kitty woke up in her feather bed, and the sun was making flickering designs on the bedroom wall as it filtered through the moving leaves of the big elm outside the window. Kitty put on a clean cotton dress that still smelled like home because she hadn't worn it yet in Norwood. She took her anklets filled with nickels from the drawer. "I'll only be able to take one at a time," she said to herself, emptying the nickels into an old purse that Aunt Katie had said she could have. "After these are gone, I'll come home and get the rest."

Kitty made her bed and brushed her teeth. Her stomach felt queasy, the way it did before she went to the dentist or had to recite in class. I've got to win him, she thought, running down the steps to the kitchen.

"How soon can we buy tickets at the bazaar?" asked Kitty.

Aunt Katie looked up from rolling more pie crust. "Tickets?" she said.

"Tickets for the dog."

"*Ach,* you don't want a dog. We're going to Mass now, just as soon as I get through with the pies."

When the last pie was out of the oven, Aunt Katie brushed the flour off her hands and swept the kitchen floor. She put on her Sunday dress and pinned her hat on in front of the mirror. Then, picking up her folded apron and her purse and Sunday missal, she called loudly, "Are you ready, Pa?"

Grandpa came into the room with his good black suit on. He was wearing a vest and a white shirt with a stiffly starched collar and cuffs, and a bow tie and suspenders. He had shaved, and his mustache was trimmed. He hung up his razor strap in the kitchen.

"You carry two pies, Kitty, and I'll carry two," said Aunt Katie.

The three of them started down the alley past Betsy's house. Betsy was probably still sleeping, thought Kitty. People from the country were already driving up in front of the church, and many more people were walking toward the church and waving to one another.

"There he is!" said Kitty. "Damien is in his pen in the yard!"

"We'll take these pies right down to the kitchen before Mass," said Aunt Katie.

Damien saw Kitty and began to bark. He tipped his head to the side and began to whine. Kitty took the pies downstairs and then ran up quickly and threw her arms around Damien's neck. "Just a little while yet," whis-

47

pered Kitty. "After Mass I'll buy the tickets!"

Kitty and Aunt Katie and Grandpa climbed the steps and entered the church with the others. They dipped their hands in the holy-water font and made the sign of the cross, then walked up the wooden aisle to the pew with Grandpa's name on it. They genuflected and knelt down on the kneeler. The sun was coming through the stained-glass window and splashing spots of color on Kitty's dress. It was a beautiful day for the bazaar.

"Dominus vobiscum!" said Father Wallace as he turned to the congregation and put his arms out.

"Et cum spiritu tuo," replied the altar boys.

Kitty couldn't wait until the Mass was over. To make time go faster, she graded the hats of all the women who sat in front of her. At the Communion, she could see even more hats as they came past her in line. Kitty had begun to do that at home, because some hats were so attractive, with colored feathers and large bright flowers and bunches of fruit, that she felt they deserved some notice. They were so much more interesting to look at than those that were plain and drab, with dingy black veiling over gray felt. If a hat was especially bright and attractive, it got an A. If it was a very drab hat, it got a D. If it was extremely ugly, it got an F. There weren't too many F's. On an average Sunday, most of the hats draw C's. What made it fun was the unexpected surprise of an outstandingly striking hat which merited an A.

When it was time for the sermon, Father Wallace introduced a missionary priest from Africa. The priest was wearing a white robe with a hood, and a brown cord around his waist. He told them about the poor people in Africa and how they didn't have enough food or clothes or medicine, and how the missionaries had no school or church but taught the children outside under a tree, even when it rained. Kitty sat up and listened.

"It only costs ten cents to feed a poor African child rice for a week, but do you think they have ten cents?"

There was silence in the church. Kitty was thinking of all the food downstairs in the basement. The smell was coming up the stairs into the church. She was thinking of the nickels people would spend playing bingo. In the silence and with the windows open, the sound of the last-minute hammering of the workmen rose to her ears.

"NO!" said the missionary, banging his fist down on the pulpit. "My friends, the people in the jungles of Africa do not have ten cents, and they don't have any rice. What can you do about it? You in this prosperous farm community of Minnesota? Well, for five dollars you can adopt a pagan baby and feed it for a year." He paused to nod his head. "You will receive in the mail a picture of your baby and the baby's name, and if the child is old enough, he will write to you from Africa, telling you how you changed his life. Just put five dollars in the envelope in your pew, and write your name and address on it, and a child in Africa will be grateful for your generosity. God bless you."

The missionary swept down from the pulpit. Kitty had tears in her eyes. She knew about pagan babies. During Lent, every boy and girl at her school was given a small cardboard box in which to save pennies that weren't spent on candy or gum, and at the end of Lent Sister Ursuline collected them. Then they put all the money together, and sometimes there was enough to buy a pagan baby. The baby's picture hung on the bulletin board, and they prayed for it every morning before the flag salute. But no one Kitty knew had ever had a pagan baby all her own. What fun to have her very own pagan baby! When it grew up, it would write to her and they would be friends and maybe Kitty could go to Africa to visit it. Or it could come to St. Paul and live with

Kitty. Kitty could share her room. Her mother couldn't turn away a pagan baby, she felt sure. It would wipe its feet and not touch the walls or curtains. Kitty could tell it about her mother's rules. Her mind spun with possibilities.

She shook her purse. She had exactly five dollars in her anklet. It seemed to be a coincidence. And she had five dollars at Aunt Katie's in the other anklet. Kitty's father always said, "You can't have your cake and eat it too," but Kitty never believed it. Whenever they had cake for dessert, she would always eat some of hers right away and save the rest. She had five dollars for the pagan baby and five dollars for Damien. Why couldn't she have both?

The organ music was playing, and the ushers came to the front with velvet-lined baskets on long sticks, to take up the collection. Kitty picked up the envelope and wrote her name and address clearly on the front. All these nickels won't ever fit, she thought in panic.

The usher was starting down the aisle, reaching in each pew with the basket. People were sealing envelopes all around her.

"I know!" cried Kitty, in such a loud whisper that Grandpa turned and looked over her head. Kitty took out her anklet with the money and untied the knot in it. She put the envelope inside the sock and tied it up again, just as the usher passed the basket in front of Aunt Katie. He was about to pull it back again, because children didn't usually buy pagan babies, but Kitty reached past Aunt Katie and put the sock full of nickels into the basket. It was so heavy that the basket dropped down almost to Aunt Katie's lap, but the usher got another grip on the handle and withdrew it carefully.

"*Mein Gott,* what was that, Kitty?" whispered Aunt Katie, moving her fingers along her rosary beads.

"Money for a pagan baby," said Kitty proudly. "Five dollars."

Aunt Katie frowned and went back to her

Hail Mary's. Grandpa was reading his German prayer book with the big letters and didn't look up.

Kitty felt warm and generous as they walked out into the bright sunshine from the dim church. What a day this was! She owned a baby all her own! And after dinner, she would own a dog. Five dollars would buy one hundred chances, and no one else would take nearly that many chances on Damien.

Four

The Church Bazaar

Betsy was sitting on her steps waiting for Kitty to come out of church. She came running over to meet her.

"You'll never guess what!" said Kitty, and she told Betsy about buying the baby. "That's still one hundred chances," she added.

"No one will buy one hundred chances," said Betsy. "He's your dog. I know he is."

Aunt Katie went downstairs with the other women to cook, while Grandpa sat in the shade on a bench, smoking and talking with the other men.

"I'll be with Betsy," called Kitty. Aunt

Katie waved and said dinner was at twelve o'clock.

"Let's go get my money!"

The girls ran through Betsy's yard and around Aunt Katie's chicken coop and in the back door. It was quiet in the house, with only the sound of the clock ticking. It still smelled like fresh pie, and the sun was sparkling on the red geraniums in the windows.

"Just a minute," called Kitty as she ran upstairs and took her other anklet out of her drawer. She put it into her purse and ran back down the steps to Betsy. "Let's be the first ones for tickets," she said.

They ran back to the church, and now there was a man selling chances on Damien. He stood in front of a table that was set up beside the pen, and was calling, "Win a fine hunting dog. Right here, this fine dog, only a nickel a chance!"

Kitty and Betsy ran up to the table, and Kitty said, "One hundred chances, please."

She dumped the nickels out of her sock on

to the table. Surprised, the man said, "Hey, girlie, what did you do, rob a bank?"

Kitty thought fast. She couldn't tell a member of the church about the slot machine. "I saved them," she said.

That wasn't a lie. She could have spent them on ice cream or another pagan baby, but she hadn't. She had saved them for Damien. No one asked how long she had saved them.

The man counted out the nickels and put them in piles, just as Kitty had done the day she won them. He shook his head. "That's a lot of chances," he said.

Kitty nodded. "I'm going to win the dog."

"You probably are," said the man, counting out one hundred chances. "It will take you all day to write your name on them," he laughed.

"I'll fill out half," said Betsy.

The girls picked up two pencils and sat on the church steps, writing Kitty's name over and over.

"My arm aches," said Kitty when they were almost through.

"Just a few more," said Betsy.

In a half-hour the girls had signed all the tickets, and Kitty walked over to the table and handed them to the man. He put them in a big wire basket with a door on the side and a handle on the end. Then he latched the door and turned the handle. Kitty's chances mixed in with the other few names inside. "The drawing is at two o'clock," he said. "Be sure to be here."

"We will," said Kitty, as she and Betsy knelt down and rubbed Damien's neck. "It's okay, fella, we'll come and get you at two o'clock."

Damien wagged his tail, and Betsy gave him part of a cookie she had in her pocket.

"What will we do until two o'clock?" groaned Kitty. "That will take forever."

"We'll eat dinner," volunteered Betsy. "It's almost noon."

"I'm not a bit hungry," said Kitty. "I'm too nervous to eat."

"I want to get in line before the crowd," said Betsy, heading for the basement door. Although Betsy was German Lutheran, she attended all the dinners and other functions at the Catholic church, partly because it was so close and partly because she was a friend of Aunt Katie and Kitty. "Our church hardly ever has dinners," she said, "and we never have a bingo."

The girls were almost the first ones in line to be seated, and Aunt Katie waved them up front where Grandpa would be sitting. She herself never ate until the dinner was over, she was so busy waiting on tables and slicing up meat.

"If we eat slowly, we won't have so long to wait," said Kitty.

"We have to play bingo before all the good prizes are gone," said Betsy.

"Who are all those dirty little kids over there?" asked Kitty.

Betsy looked at the family coming in. The father was a large, red-faced farmer with manure and hay from the barn still on his boots.

The mother appeared to be expecting a baby very soon. She looked cross and tired. Several small children with runny noses clung to her skirt. The little girls' dresses were homemade and old-fashioned, and the boys' hair was long and stiff. They wore short pants.

"They're the Zachmans, from out west of town," said Betsy, reaching for a carrot stick.

"The girls' dresses are too long," said Kitty.

"They are p-o-o-r," said Betsy, spelling it.

"I'll bet the kids at school tease them," said Kitty, suddenly sympathetic.

"They don't go to school."

"Why don't they go to school?"

"They don't speak English. Two of them went once to the first grade, but the principal sent them home after a couple of weeks—it was awful, no one could understand them, and they couldn't understand the teachers and the kids. Kids called 'em Nazis."

Kitty watched them walk to a table all alone and sit down. The children seemed frightened.

"Maybe they are Nazis," said Kitty softly.

"Naw, they just can't talk anything but German."

"Maybe they're spies." Kitty had a vivid imagination, her mother said.

"I don't think so," said Betsy, eating another carrot stick and losing interest in the Zachmans.

Grandpa came and sat down across from Kitty and Betsy. A moment later the women began putting dishes of hot meat and potatoes and vegetables on the tables.

"Eat slowly," whispered Kitty, nibbling a pickle.

"All the food will be gone," said Betsy, heaping her plate with mashed potatoes.

Even though Kitty dawdled over her food, her plate was soon empty, and the women cleared the table and brought dessert. The girls drank the last of their milk and noticed that the tables were nearly empty. "We can't sit here forever," said Betsy.

"Kitty! Betsy!" Aunt Katie was waving

them into the kitchen with a dish towel. "Come dry the dishes here!"

Kitty looked at the clock on the wall over the steps. It was one o'clock. The girls picked up towels and began to wipe glasses and plates.

"Wow! I never saw so many dishes!" said Betsy. "Look at all that silverware!"

The women were laughing and talking among themselves. They seemed to enjoy bending over the hot, steamy sink, scouring pans and wiping tables.

"I can't see why they think this is so much fun," said Kitty.

Emma, who lived across the alley from Betsy, was wiping the steam from her glasses with one hand and slapping her knee with the other. She laughed so hard that her glasses got steamed up all over again.

"They're all friends," said Betsy.

Kitty tried to picture herself grown up, with her friends Margaret Mary and Eileen, washing millions of dishes in a church basement. In her mind she could see Margaret Mary with a nice clean apron on and a smile on her face. But the picture got dim when she tried to see herself or Eileen. Eileen would never be in a church basement when she was grown up. And she'd never wash or dry a dish, even her own. I might be there, thought Kitty to herself, but I wouldn't be laughing. I'd be there because I can never say no. She thought of all the things she'd done that she hated doing, just because she could never say no.

"Let's go," she whispered to Betsy. "They are having such a good time they will never notice we are gone."

Kitty was right. They hung their wet dish towels over the towel rack and ran up the back church steps that came out in the cemetery. They turned the corner of the church and joined the crowds of people milling around the bingo table. "B 10!" shouted the announcer loudly into a megaphone. "B 10!" His voice sounded hollow and professional like the man outside the sideshows in the midway at the state fair. Kitty could feel shivers run up and down her arms. This was a very exciting day.

"Let's go and look at Damien," she said. The girls went to the front churchyard. People were gathered around the puppy's pen, poking fingers through the chicken wire to pat his nose. More people were in line, still buying chances.

"Look," said Kitty. "Look at that wire basket with the tickets. It's full now."

The man opened the door on the side and put in three more tickets. Then he turned the handle to shake them up.

"I didn't know so many people would want a dog," said Kitty.

"He's purebred," said Betsy. "Purebred Labradors are good hunters."

Kitty didn't care a thing about how purebred Damien was. She wished now that he was a mongrel, so that no one would want him.

"He probably has papers and everything," said Betsy.

The girls sat down on the grass to wait. "It's almost two o'clock," said Kitty.

Suddenly the man behind the ticket counter held up his hands. He picked up a megaphone and said, "Last chance to win this purebred black Labrador hunting dog." He looked around at the people sitting on the grass and standing beside Damien's pen. "Last chance," he called again, waving tickets above his head. "Step right up and win yourself this dog, folks."

Suddenly, from the back of the crowd, a man in a shabby suit came forward.

"That's Mr. Zachman!" said Betsy, poking Kitty. "What would he want with a dog?"

Mr. Zachman held out one nickel on the palm of his hand.

"Yes, sir," said the ticket man, handing Mr. Zachman a ticket. "Write your name right there," he said, handing him a pencil.

Mr. Zachman looked puzzled. He walked away with his ticket.

"Your name, sir, we need your name on the

ticket for the drawing," called the ticket man.

Mr. Zachman kept walking.

"He doesn't understand English," said Betsy.

Suddenly Kitty stood up. Mr. Zachman was right beside her. *"Namen,"* she said, pointing to his ticket. Kitty didn't know much German, but she had heard Aunt Katie say "name" to people. *"Namen!"*

Betsy looked up in surprise. She didn't know that Kitty knew any German at all.

Kitty led Mr. Zachman back up to the ticket counter while everyone watched. She picked up the pencil and handed it to him. *"Namen,"* she said again.

Mr. Zachman looked sad. He shook his head.

Kitty looked at Betsy. She gestured with her finger, urging her to come up. When she got there, Kitty whispered, "Isn't that how you say 'name'?"

Betsy nodded. She put her mouth close to Kitty's ear. "But he can't *write,*" she whispered.

Kitty's eyes opened wide. She had gone this far; there was nothing else to do. "Here," she said to Mr. Zachman, taking the ticket from his hand. She picked up the pencil and wrote carefully, "Mr. Zachman," then she handed the slip of paper to the ticket man. Mr. Zachman walked away with an absent look on his face.

The girls sat down on the grass. "Why did you do that?" said Betsy. "Everyone's looking at us."

"We couldn't let him waste his nickel," said Kitty. "He only bought one chance." It had all happened so fast that Kitty hadn't thought about what she'd done. Her first impulse was to help someone who couldn't even speak English.

"Now!" said the ticket man. "We will have the drawing to see who wins this fine black dog!"

Damien jumped up and down in the pen. He was wagging his tail. Kitty crossed her fingers and closed her eyes. Betsy did too. The man was turning and turning the wire basket.

"Around and around and around she goes," said the man dramatically. "And where she stops, nobody knows . . ."

Betsy opened her eyes for a minute. "Those aren't even getting mixed up, because the basket is so full," she said.

"The winner is—" called the man, stopping the basket. He opened the door and picked a ticket out. He looked at it carefully. "The winner is—" he said again.

Kitty was afraid to hear. She had to win. She had more tickets than anyone else.

"—MR. ZACHMAN!" said the man.

Kitty opened her eyes. She uncrossed her fingers. She couldn't believe her ears.

Betsy stared at the ticket man with her mouth wide open. "But you didn't mix those up!" she said loudly. "That was the last ticket you put in, and it was on top! They didn't even get mixed up, that thing was so full." Betsy was on her feet now.

The ticket man appeared not to hear her. He was looking straight ahead.

"Mr. Zachman," he called again. "Mr. Zachman has won himself a fine purebred hunting dog!"

Kitty's eyes started to water. She had been all ready to go and put her arms around Damien and take him home. Betsy was shaking her fist at the man.

As Mr. Zachman wandered up to the dog pen, Kitty got up and ran. She ran across the street and up the alley. She kept running until she got to Aunt Katie's house and went in the back door and slammed the screen. She threw herself down at the dining-room table and cried.

In a few minutes Betsy came in. "It wasn't fair," she said to Kitty. "You had all those chances, and they were all on the bottom. He only had one and it was on top because it was the last one in. That wasn't fair." Betsy's face was red.

Kitty wiped her face with the back of her hand. "And *I* wrote his name on it!" she said.

"It was my fault he won at all! He had one ticket, and I wrote his name on it!"

"I think we should tell Father Wallace," said Betsy. "A church should be fair."

The girls sat and listened to the clock tick. It struck two-thirty. In the distance they could hear people in the churchyard, laughing and talking.

"I'll never have a dog," moaned Kitty. "My best chance, and I lost. I'll never have a dog of my own in my whole life."

"You should have bought your tickets last," said Betsy, still angry over the injustice of the situation. "You bought them first and they stayed on the bottom. Mr. Zachman just wanders up at the last minute with his one darn nickel, and he almost walks off with his ticket, and he wins Damien." Here Betsy imitated Mr. Zachman walking up to the counter slowly and walking away absently with the ticket in his hand. "But no, you had to get up and help him, yet! *Gott in Himmel!*"

Betsy looked so funny, walking like Mr.

Zachman and then showing how Kitty had jumped up and led him back and signed the ticket, that Kitty began to laugh.

"What's so funny?" said Betsy.

"You are," said Kitty. "Well, anyway, I gave a lot of money to the church today. And I have a pagan baby."

"You can name him Damien," said Betsy, and Kitty smiled at the idea of a baby named Damien, even though she felt more like crying.

The back screen door slammed. Aunt Katie came in with her empty pie tins and bags of leftover food. "You home already, ain't so," she said.

"I didn't win the dog," said Kitty.

"*Ach,* who wants a dog?" she said, putting the food in the pantry.

Five

Off to the Farm

The day after the bazaar, Kitty and Betsy went to the churchyard with Aunt Katie to help Father Wallace and Emily and some of the workmen clean up the grounds. They picked up paper and balloons and pop bottles and watched the men take down the bingo stand and Damien's pen. Kitty found it hard to believe that only yesterday she had been happy here among the laughing crowds on the church lawn. By afternoon all traces of the bazaar were gone. Father Wallace was saying the rosary out loud as he clipped the weeds around the monument in the cemetery, and Kitty and Betsy went home.

Kitty tried not to think about Damien and the raffle, because then she remembered that that had been her only chance in the world to own a dog, and it made her sad. So she played Mass on the chicken coop with Betsy and helped Aunt Katie in the garden, and the days passed quickly.

One morning, while Kitty was still in bed, there was a knock on the door downstairs. She could hear Aunt Katie talking to someone. Kitty got out of bed and looked out of her window. In the backyard at the edge of the alley stood a horse hitched to a farm wagon. In St. Paul she rarely saw a horse, and even in Norwood most people drove cars unless they were going to the feed mill or the grain elevator. When they came to someone's house, they never drove a horse.

Aunt Katie was rushing around downstairs, and before long she opened the door to the stairs and called up, "Kitty! Kitty, we're going to the farm now. Get dressed and pack some things in your grip."

The farm? Kitty had forgotten about going to the farm. Aunt Katie had to cook and care for the children while the mother had a baby. Kitty remembered. "Coming!" she called.

She ran to the storeroom and got out her suitcase and put her underwear and socks into it. She wondered if she should take her good dress to the farm. Yes, she would need at least one good dress. Kitty wondered how long it took to get over having a baby. She put in her silver bracelet and her hat, just in case they were there until Sunday. She began to feel excited. There would be animals on the farm, and grass and flowers and the hayloft to play in. She remembered pictures she had seen of farms, with ropes in the hayloft to swing on and horses to ride. She and Aunt Katie would mind the children and feed the baby and bake cakes together. It would be like playing house. She put her talcum powder into her suitcase and folded her taffeta dress with tissue paper between so it wouldn't wrinkle. She brushed her teeth and washed her face and decided to wear the dress she'd worn the day before. It was still clean. Everything raced through Kitty's mind all at once. It was too early to say goodbye to Betsy, who would still be sleeping. She wondered if the farmer came to town often. Maybe she could ride back to see Betsy and tell her all about keeping house and riding horses, and maybe Betsy could even come out one day to visit.

"Kitty!" called Aunt Katie. "We are ready to go."

Kitty snapped the latch on her suitcase and ran down the steps. Aunt Katie was talking to Grandpa in the parlor. "You go to Emma's at noon, Pa. You have dinner at Emma's. She'll set a place for you. Kitty, you run over to Emma and tell her we're leaving and to set a place for Pa."

Kitty ran through Betsy's yard and across the alley to Emma's. Emma was a distant cousin of Aunt Katie's and Kitty's father. The thing Kitty remembered most about Emma was that last summer Aunt Katie had said,

"Wait 'til you see what Emma has." Kitty and her mother and father had crossed the alley to Emma's house, thinking maybe she had a new kitchen table or a new icebox, and Aunt Katie had taken them into Emma's bedroom, where she picked up a pink blanket from the bed—and inside was a baby. A real, live baby. "Whose is it?" Kitty had asked. Her mother and father had looked embarrassed, and Aunt Katie and Emma had laughed and laughed the way they had at the bazaar, and Emma had turned red and looked at the floor, and no one had said anything. So Kitty asked again, "Whose is it?" Emma said, "Guess," and sure enough, it turned out to be Emma's baby. Kitty had been about to open her mouth to say Emma was too old to have babies, but everyone had been congratulating her and talking at once and passing the baby around.

Emma and her husband had only one other child, and he wasn't a child any more but twenty years old and overseas in the Navy. Pictures of him in his Navy uniform were

hanging on the wall in the bedroom and standing on the dresser and on the piano. "Wait 'til
Leo comes home and sees his little sister!"
Emma had said. "We wrote that we had a
surprise for him when he comes home on fur-
lough, but we haven't heard a thing. Not a
thing for ten months," she had explained.
Emma had laughed, thinking of showing the
baby to Leo. "He'll be so surprised!" she'd
said.

"He'll faint," Kitty had said, and her mother
had nudged her to be quiet.

Now that very baby was toddling around
outside under the clothesline, and Emma was
hanging diapers and had clothespins in her
mouth, and Leo still hadn't come home.

"*Wie geht's!*" said Emma. "You are up
early this morning."

"We're going to the farm, Emma. We have
to leave for the farm right away. Will you give
Grandpa dinner at noon?"

"*Ja,* sure, you tell the old man to come over.
we'll set a place for him." She wiped her fore-

head. It was going to be a hot day. "So Agatha had her baby, did she? Did you hear what it was, Kitty?"

"No," said Kitty. "I don't know about the baby. But we have to hurry out to the farm."

Emma waved. "You send Pa over," she said.

Kitty ran back down the gravel alley. Aunt Katie had Kitty's grip and was climbing up onto the farmer's wagon. Her hair was already coming out of the pug she'd drawn it back into, and the farmer's shirt was dark on his back and chest where it was wet.

Kitty held onto the sides of the wagon and pulled herself up, being careful not to get her dress or anklets dirty. She brushed off a spot beside Aunt Katie and sat down, full of anticipation. It was then that she looked up at the farmer and opened her mouth to say hello. But before she could say a word, she felt a strange feeling come over her. It was the same way she had felt the time she had waited and waited for St. Nicholas to come and throw candy in the back door on St. Nicholas Day. She had hidden in the stairway and waited, and when the door flew open she had looked behind the hurtling candy, expecting to see the white-haired head of St. Nick. Instead she had seen her uncle Johnny—not even dressed like St. Nicholas. Just her plain uncle with a big bag of candy. Kitty knew there must be some mistake, but she hadn't been able to tell her mother because she wasn't supposed to see St. Nicholas, or her uncle Johnny, for that matter.

Now on the farm wagon, when she looked up expecting to see a friendly farmer who would take Aunt Katie and her to a new adventure on the farm, she saw instead the face of Mr. Zachman. At first Kitty couldn't remember where she'd seen it before. She knew she had seen it somewhere, and then suddenly she remembered Damien and the ticket and signing his name. Aunt Katie was chattering away to Mr. Zachman in German, and Mr. Zachman wasn't saying anything. He was just nodding his head and shaking the reins on the horse as they started down the alley.

When there was a pause in Aunt Katie's German, Kitty whispered into her ear: "Why is Mr. Zachman driving this wagon?"

Aunt Katie looked surprised. "*Ach,* the baby, Kitty. Agatha Zachman had a boy this morning."

"*Zachmans'?*" shouted Kitty. "We are going to the *Zachmans'?*"

Aunt Katie was talking German again by this time, and the horse was pulling them down the gravel road that wound between fields and woods. Farther and farther away from town and Aunt Katie's house and closer and closer to the farm. Zachman's farm. Kitty couldn't say a word, and no one asked her to. She sat on the floor of the wagon and thought of Mrs. Zachman in the church basement, looking like she was going to have a baby, and all the dirty children with runny noses clinging to her with upturned eyes and stiff, bristly hair. She found herself thinking of a dirty baby. A little newborn dirty baby. Why in the world would they have another baby, Kitty wondered. They already had more than enough children. But Kitty didn't say that out loud. She remembered how quiet everyone had gotten when she had mentioned Emma's baby. For some reason adults didn't like to talk about having babies, dirty or clean. It seemed all right to talk about the baby itself, but not how or why it was there.

"How much does the baby weigh?" said Kitty. That was a safe subject; she had heard her mother ask people how much babies weighed. And if she was going to have to be a guest at the Zachmans' house (and it looked like she was), she would have to talk to them.

Aunt Katie turned to Kitty and waved a limp hand in the air. "*Ach,* how would they know how much it weighed? It's a live boy. A breech baby, but a fine boy."

A breech baby. Kitty wondered what in the world *breech* was. A breech boy. She knew what breeches were. Surely the baby wasn't born wearing breeches! Maybe it was a birth-mark. She had seen a boy on the streetcar once with a purple mark all over one side of his face. When she had asked her mother, her mother had said, "Sshh, that's a birthmark."

That must be it. The Zachmans' baby must have a purple face. Kitty felt sad. The Zachman children had enough things wrong with them as it was, without having purple faces. She closed her eyes and said a prayer for the baby. She prayed that the purple breech birthmark would go away and he'd be spared this terrible affliction. "Amen."

Kitty had lost her anticipation for the farm. The sun beat down on the wagon and made the tops of their heads hot. The dust from the horse's hooves and the wagon wheels rose around them and settled on Kitty's wet arms. She could feel the dust between her teeth and on the white collar of her dress. Mr. Zachman stared straight ahead, all red in the face, looking just like he had the day he had won Damien.

Damien. She would see Damien again. Perhaps she could rescue him and give him a good home after all. Her spirits began to lift. Maybe it wouldn't be so bad, thought Kitty. Maybe the Zachmans had just looked bad that day, and they had other clothes, clean clothes. Maybe when she got to know them, and stayed at their house, they would be fun. Maybe she could teach them English, and they could teach her German, and they would laugh together and all hold hands and run out to the barn to see the animals. Well, maybe not hold hands, reflected Kitty. They would at least have animals. All farms had animals. And a farmhouse. Farmhouses were large and white and had gathered curtains at the window and a piano. The farmhouses Kitty had seen in pictures had a piano in the parlor. She imagined everyone gathered around the piano in the evening, singing and smiling and maybe eating popcorn. Then they would all help with the chores (Kitty would gather eggs herself) and go up the open staircase to bed, blowing kisses over the banister. The bed in the guestroom would have a feather mattress. Kitty knew that farmhouses had feather beds, made from the feathers of all the ducks and chickens. Even the Zachmans must have feather beds. Kitty frowned. She felt doubtful.

Mr. Zachman pulled on one of the horse's reins. The horse turned from the gravel road onto a dirt road with grass growing in the middle, between the wagon wheels. They drove through some large, muddy puddles and over some bumpy rocks in the road, and up ahead Kitty could see a house. Not a big white house but a gray peeling house, with old tires in the yard, a rusty plow beside them, and chickens on the front porch. The horse stopped when Mr. Zachman shouted something in German to him and pulled on the reins.

"Here we are. Bring your grip, Kitty," said Aunt Katie.

Kitty wanted to stay right where she was and tell the horse to turn around and go back to town, but she stood up and followed Aunt Katie into the house. She blinked when she went in from the bright sunlight, and when she could see again, it seemed as if there were children everywhere—the same dreary, dirty children she had seen in church, wearing the same clothes. Instead of hanging onto their mother, they were hanging onto corners and furniture and each other. The room looked like church to Kitty, with statues everywhere, with vigil lights burning in front of them and blessed palm stuck behind them.

Aunt Katie bustled around, patting the children's stiff, bristly hair and talking with smiles in German. The children lifted their eyes and answered in German monosyllables. Then Aunt Katie hurried upstairs to Mrs. Zachman and the breech baby. Kitty stood in her stiffly starched dress which, even though she'd worn it before, looked remarkably clean in the Zachmans' parlor. She held her suitcase at her side. The children stared.

"Hi," said Kitty.

The children cast their eyes to the floor. A cat walked along and rubbed on Kitty's legs, and Kitty ran up the stairs in the direction she'd seen Aunt Katie go.

"Aunt Katie?" called Kitty. "Aunt Katie, where are you?"

"Sshh," said Aunt Katie, coming out of one of the rooms at the end of a dark hall.

"Where should I put my suitcase?"

"*Ach,* put it in the bedroom, here." She flung her hand toward a door across from the room she had just left. Kitty looked inside. Instead of the feather bed she had pictured, she saw an old metal bed frame with a straw mattress on it and a faded blanket in a heap at the foot. On the cracked wall were two crucifixes and a picture of the Sacred Heart. A pail of water with a dipper hanging beside it stood on a wooden chair, and flies walked slowly around the edge. Kitty shuddered. Her suitcase looked new and shiny and attractive and entirely out of place when she set it near the bed. She looked around for a hanger, to hang up her taffeta dress. All she saw was a row of hooks on the wall, and they had overalls hanging from them, their cuffs covered with manure from the barn.

"Is this my room?" she called to Aunt Katie. Aunt Katie put her head around the corner of the doorway. "What is it, child?"

"Is this my room?" Kitty repeated.

"The girls sleep in there."

The girls were sliding around the doorjamb and leaning on the walls. They stared at Kitty again. It looked to Kitty as if there were dozens of them, though there were only three.

"Where is *my* room?" demanded Kitty.

"Right here, the girls sleep right here."

"There's only one bed," said Kitty.

"Two at the top, and two at the bottom."

"In one bed?" shrieked Kitty. "All of us in one bed?" Kitty had never heard of such a thing. When Margaret Mary or Eileen stayed overnight, she shared her double bed, and even that seemed crowded. Eileen had twin beds in her room.

Kitty thought of nighttime. She thought of that straw bed and those silent girls staring at her. She thought of her clean pajamas with embroidered rosebuds, the ones that her mother had ironed, and that smelled like her house in St. Paul and now a little bit like Aunt Katie's. She thought of those pajamas in that bed. The thing she couldn't think of at all was herself in that bed with those children. Ever. She'd die first.

She picked up her suitcase and ran down the steps and outside. She kept running 'til she was away from the house and behind the barn. Then she put her suitcase on the ground and sat on it. "Never, never never," she said.

Kitty looked at the trees and hills and flowers. It was better outside, away from that awful house and those dismal children. Maybe she could sleep outside, on the grass. No, a whole week of sleeping on the ground would be too long. It might rain.

Kitty sat on her suitcase a long time. The sun was overhead and the church bell was ringing when she heard Aunt Katie call her name.

"Kitty, Kitty, *komm essen!*"

Kitty didn't want to think of dinner. She wasn't hungry, and she couldn't go back in that house.

"KITTY?"

She heard the back door slam as Aunt Katie called out to her. She wondered how Aunt Katie even noticed she was gone, with so many children milling around. Kitty picked up her suitcase and walked back to the house. Mr. Zachman, coming in from the barn, tipped his hat and wiped his boots on the manure scraper by the back door. Bits of hay and dirt still clung to his overalls, but he walked into the kitchen and drank a dipperful of water from the bucket, and then poured some into a bowl to wash his face.

Aunt Katie was bustling about the wood stove. She set a large kettle of potatoes in the middle of the wooden table. They had not been peeled, and were steaming in their red jackets. Kitty had never seen so many potatoes. Aunt Katie then sat on a wooden chair at one end of the table, and Mr. Zachman at the other, and all the children piled in between them. Slipping onto the chair Aunt Katie pointed to, Kitty bowed her head and made the sign of the cross as everyone prayed in German. Then, as if given a signal, everyone put his fork into a potato and lifted it to his plate and cut it up and began to eat. When the kettle was empty, Aunt Katie took it off the table and replaced it with one just like it that had been boiling on the back of the stove. Kitty felt the same way she had in the bedroom, as though she were in the wrong place by accident. All alone, where she didn't fit. Everyone but her appeared to love the potatoes. Everyone but her spoke German. No one but her looked upset.

When the kettle was empty the second time, they all bowed their heads and prayed again, then stood up and scraped the wooden chairs back on the linoleum floor and cleared the table.

"Take the scraps to the chickens," said Aunt Katie to Kitty as she scraped the peelings onto a plate. Kitty walked out the back door to the barnyard and set the plate down on the ground. She felt the day would never end. But what good would it do if it did end? Then there would be that awful bed in that awful house with people who couldn't understand her and who probably hated her. It wasn't the day that had to end, it was the whole week. Tears came to Kitty's eyes when she thought about it. There were no electric lights, and it would soon be pitch dark. Besides being lonely, Kitty felt scared. She knew the Zachmans didn't have a bathroom—she had seen pots under the bed. How could she go to the bathroom with three other people in the room? Kitty's stomach began to ache. She thought of her grandpa sitting down at Emma's table right now, with plates that were not chipped and people who spoke English and who had meat and vegetables and cabbage salad for dinner. She thought of her room at Aunt Katie's, and Betsy next door. Kitty counted the hours until supper, then she thought of the potatoes again and of the moment when she would have to go to that bedroom, and she began to cry harder.

She heard something behind her and turned around. Leaning on the barn and pointing were the Zachman children. They were pointing at her and giggling. *They were laughing at her.*

Six

Kitty Runs Away

Kitty got up and ran. She ran past the barn, past the house, and down the dirt road. She ran and ran and didn't look back. She was all the way to the gravel road before she stopped to rest and wipe her eyes. All she could think of was getting away from the Zachmans. Nothing else mattered. She turned right at the gravel road and kept running, and the farther she ran, the better she felt. It didn't matter if it was miles, she'd run forever 'til she got to Aunt Katie's or to St. Paul. Nobody could make her stay at the farm.

Before long, Kitty felt so much better she began to hum. Cars and farm wagons passed her on the road. The people waved and looked friendly and clean, as if they spoke English and ate other food besides potatoes. Kitty could feel her skin getting sunburned. Her shoes were white with dust from the gravel and she was thirsty and she'd forgotten her suitcase, but none of that mattered. Nothing could make her feel bad now. She was away from Zachmans' at last. It seemed like she'd been there for a week.

Just when Kitty thought she was never ever going to come to the end of the road or see anything but fields again in her life, she noticed a church steeple ahead. It was Aunt Katie's church, and her house was three doors away! As she got closer, she could read the clock in the steeple: three thirty-five. It had only been a little over five hours!

Suddenly Kitty remembered something. In the whole long day she'd been at the Zachmans', she hadn't seen the breech baby! And she also had not seen Damien.

As Kitty came to Aunt Katie's yard, she had

a feeling of trespassing. Just this morning she had climbed happily up onto the farm wagon and left for a trip, a visit to a farm where she was supposed to be right now. She was not supposed to be here. Everyone knew she was in the country with Aunt Katie.

Kitty wiped the gravel dust off her shoes and climbed up Aunt Katie's steps. She turned the doorknob and went in. No one ever locked their doors in Norwood. Grandpa, his glasses down on his nose, was asleep in his chair, with the German newspaper over his chest. His mouth was open and he was snoring. Kitty wondered if people snored in different languages. It seemed to her that Grandpa was snoring in German.

Everything was just as Aunt Katie had left it—the geraniums in their saucers on the windowsills, the tablecloth from supper on the dining-room table. Kitty wondered what to do. She couldn't just run over and play with Betsy like on any ordinary day. She couldn't go to Emma's. Emma would ask a lot of questions.

She didn't belong in Norwood today, but she surely didn't belong at the Zachmans'. Kitty didn't feel that she belonged anywhere. She had left the house with such great excitement, not expecting to see it again for a week. And here she was, back the same day, without time for it even to look different. But it did. It looked clean and quiet and cozy after the Zachmans'.

Kitty felt uneasy. She went out and sat on the back steps. What will I say when people see that I'm home? she thought. She tried to think of things to tell people. "I can say I got sick and it was catchy and I had to leave." Then Emma would want to take her to the doctor. "I'll say I forgot something important." Then they'd say, "What is it?" and send her back. No matter what she said, they'd know the truth when Aunt Katie came home. Well, she sure couldn't say, "The Zachmans are messy, dirty people with lots of kids who can't talk English and eat potatoes all the time and I hate them."

A car drove down the alley. The driver waved. Kitty waved back. A little later a neighbor on her way downtown called, "Hi, Kitty!" and Kitty answered. They aren't even surprised I'm here, she thought. They act like I belong here. Kitty felt a little braver. She went in the house and got a piece of chalk and played hopscotch on the sidewalk. After a while her grandpa opened the screen door and stepped outside. He took out his little drawstring bag of tobacco and filled his pipe, packing the tobacco down carefully with his thumb. Then he took out his box of long wooden matches and lit the pipe.

"Hi, Grandpa," said Kitty.

Grandpa stared straight ahead.

"I know I'm supposed to be in the country, but I came back for something." Kitty tried to make her voice sound ordinary, like it was an everyday thing that she ran away from where she was.

Grandpa sat on the edge of the cistern and crossed his legs. He puffed on his pipe and stared out over the rows of beans and potatoes in the garden. Kitty wondered if he had heard her. He took a watch out of his pocket and looked at it. "Where is Kathryn?" he said to Kitty.

"She's at Zachmans'," said Kitty. "You go to Emma's to eat."

Kitty's grandpa got up and headed slowly for the alley. When he was almost there, he turned and looked at her. *"Komm essen,"* he said, and crooked his elbow in the direction of Emma's house.

Kitty was surprised. He did know she was real, after all. Wasn't he going to ask what she was doing there? Wasn't he going to ask if Aunt Katie knew she was gone? At home in St. Paul, Kitty's mother wanted to know where she had been if she was five minutes late coming home from school. And after supper, when she played outside, her father whistled for her to come in long before the streetlights came on. They always knew where she was.

Grandpa was waiting. Puffing on his pipe

and waiting. Kitty wondered if her mother and father knew they took such poor care of her here in Norwood. Why, she could have run clear to another town and her grandpa would have gone to Emma's by himself and never known the difference.

Kitty felt hungry. She hadn't had anything to eat since breakfast, and she'd walked a long way. She thought of Emma's supper: lunch-meat sandwiches, or veal or beef roast left over from dinner; fresh vegetables from the garden; maybe wilted lettuce with cream and vinegar and sugar. Kitty's mouth watered. If she went to Emma's, she was sure to have to explain. Emma wouldn't take this as lightly as Grandpa did. She would demand an explanation and maybe get all excited and get someone to drive her out to Zachmans' after supper. Maybe even before supper. Kitty shuddered. She wasn't going back. No one could ever make her go back there, ever again. Her stomach felt empty. She would take a chance. She would go with

Grandpa and take a chance. After all, she couldn't hide from everyone forever.

Kitty ran after Grandpa. They scraped their shoes on the scraper by Emma's back steps and opened the door. It smelled warm and cozy, a mixture of kerosene from the stove and cooking food. Emma waved a spoon. *"Wie geht's!"* she called. "Come and sit down. I've got supper here on the stove."

She smiled at Kitty, her cheeks red and rosy and her mouth turned up like it always was. Emma always looked happy. Kitty couldn't remember ever seeing her when she wasn't beaming. "You like beets, Kitty?" Emma laughed. Emma laughed and laughed, and her baby laughed and laughed, even though Kitty couldn't see anything funny about beets.

Kitty nodded. "I like beets," she said when the laughter subsided.

Emma ruffled her hair and clapped her on the back. Then she laughed some more.

How can she talk about beets when I'm not

even supposed to be here? thought Kitty.
Doesn't she know that I'm missing?

Emma was banging dishes around the pantry
and singing now. "Kitty," she called. "Will
you put another place at the table?" She
handed her a plate. "Take a chair from the
bedroom," she called.

Grandpa was already sitting at his place at the
table, smoking his pipe.

Emma, grinning, went to the door. She
was short and plump, with her hair pulled back,
wearing black oxfords and stockings rolled at
the knees. She called to Wayne, her husband:
"*Komm essen,* Wayne!"

Wayne came in the door a moment later and
washed up at the sink. After he sat down and
hung his hat on the back of his chair, they said
grace and began to eat. Kitty looked at the table
weighed down with meat and vegetables and
fresh bread. She looked at the happy baby in
the highchair, and tried to put Zachmans' and
the potatoes out of her mind. She was here now,
even if she shouldn't be and even if no one

cared that she was missing and worried about her. At least she was having a fine supper. Wayne grinned at her just like Emma had.

"And what did Agatha have, Kitty, a boy or a girl?" asked Emma, buttering a thick piece of homemade bread and spreading it with sour cream.

Well, thought Kitty, at least she does remember that I went to Zachmans' this morning. "A boy," said Kitty. "A breech boy."

"Breech?" said Emma, folding her bread in half. "Ah," she said, shaking her head and smiling, "that's no fun. No, sir, that's no fun . . . Breech," she said to her husband and baby again, as if they hadn't heard. "Did you hear that? I wonder if Agatha's all right, then." Smile.

What does she mean, *Agatha,* thought Kitty. She should worry about the poor baby, with that dreadful purple breech mark on its face forever.

Emma cleared the plates when they were through and brought in fresh strawberries over biscuits, with fresh whipped cream. Kitty enjoyed every bite and felt happy as long as she didn't think of the farm. When she did, that awful feeling in her stomach came back. She helped Emma with the dishes while Grandpa fell asleep in one of Emma's chairs, listening to war news on the radio, and then Emma put the baby to bed.

When Grandpa got out his watch and saw that it was nine o'clock, he stood up and walked toward the door.

"Bye, John," said Emma, waving a hand above her head. "Come over tomorrow if Kate is gone. You too, Kitty."

Kitty had thought of tomorrow. She wondered if Aunt Katie had missed her yet. Probably not, she told herself; no one seems to care where people are around here.

She crossed the alley with Grandpa, but as they were about to go in the house, a farm wagon pulled into the yard. Mr. Zachman was sitting at the reins. Aunt Katie was climbing down and she looked excited.

"Kitty," she called. "So you're here. I looked all over the place. Now we had to come chasing to town for you." Aunt Katie looked exasperated and hot and tired. "Come. Get on the wagon, girl." Aunt Katie turned around and motioned for Kitty to follow.

"Ohhhh, no," said Kitty. "I'm not going back to that awful farm. I'll never go back there in my life."

Aunt Katie looked surprised. *"Ach,* get on the wagon, Kitty," she said, as if that settled it.

"I'm not going," shouted Kitty. "Don't you ever hear me? I said I'm not going." Kitty felt shaky at her own courage. Her mother would have said she was sassy.

"Ach, get on the wagon." Aunt Katie was getting impatient.

"You go ahead. I'm not going."

"Where do you think you'll stay?"

"I'll stay here."

"You can't stay here, with no one to cook."

"I'll stay with Emma."

"You can't just move in with relatives. They don't want you."

Kitty thought a while. "I'll stay with Betsy," she said brightly. Betsy wouldn't mind.

"Betsy is a Protestant. You can't stay overnight with Protestants."

Kitty thought it was far better to stay with clean Protestants who spoke English and had a variety of food in their icebox than with a Catholic family that didn't. "Well, I'm not going back to the farm, and that's that." Kitty turned and walked into the house and up the stairs to her bedroom. She thought of the bedroom she could have been sleeping in at this moment, and then she thought of how sassy she had been to Aunt Katie. "I want to go home," she said out loud, and threw herself down on the feather bed without even taking off her shoes. She began to cry.

She heard voices outside in German. Then she heard the horse and wagon start off down the alley and the back screen door slam. Now she felt guilty. The breech baby and the poor mother and all the dirty Zachman children had no one to cook for them. Well, anyone should be able to cook potatoes, thought Kitty.

"Now look what you've done," said Aunt Katie, coming into the bedroom.

Kitty started to cry harder. "I want to go home. Right now. I want to go home tonight." The thought of her own house on Jefferson Avenue and her own room was too excruciating to bear. She had to go home. She belonged at home.

Aunt Katie sighed. Kitty couldn't see her, but she knew she was standing with her hands on her hips. Aunt Katie wasn't used to children who were temperamental. She tickled babies and gave children sugar cookies, and they never asked for the impossible. Like Kitty did.

"Take me home!" shouted Kitty, close to hysteria.

Aunt Katie countered by shouting louder. "How do you think I'm going to take you fifty miles tonight?"

"I want my daddy!" said Kitty, knowing that she sounded like a baby and not caring at all. Kitty liked her father best, and she knew he

would come and get her somehow. If he knew, he would come at once.

"Come. We will go downtown and call him."

Kitty sat up. She wiped her eyes. "Really?" she said.

"We can call from the hotel," said Aunt Katie. She looked as relieved as Kitty at a possible solution.

Kitty got up and combed her hair, and she and Aunt Katie started down the dark alley toward town. Grandpa was in bed, snoring.

When they got to the hotel, Aunt Katie picked up the telephone on the clerk's desk and talked to the operator for a minute. The operator lived near church and operated the telephone company from her own home.

"Reverse the charges," said Aunt Katie.

Kitty was excited now that Aunt Katie was actually getting her father on the phone. She could hear him answer. He probably wondered who was calling so late at night.

"Can you come and get Kitty?" Aunt Katie

was direct. There was a pause. *"Ach,* I think she's spoiled."

"I am *not* spoiled," shouted Kitty into the phone. "I want to come home. I want to come home right now."

Aunt Katie and Kitty's father talked some more. Then Aunt Katie said goodbye and hung up.

"Well," said Kitty. "When is he coming?"

"Saturday," said Aunt Katie.

"Saturday!" shrieked Kitty. "Saturday is ages away. I have to go home *now.*"

"He can't get away from the office," sighed Aunt Katie, sounding sadder about it than Kitty. "And your aunt Jo has no gas stamps 'til next week."

"I can take the train," said Kitty. "That's it, I'll take the train."

"By the time he sent money for a ticket, it would be Saturday anyway, child," said Aunt Katie, starting for the door. "Come, we'll go home."

Seven

Back to the Farm

Kitty and Aunt Katie walked back to the house in silence. Kitty put her pajamas on and crawled into bed and thought of how her father had betrayed her. There must be some way he could have rescued her. He must not know how bad the problem was. Surely he had never been to the Zachmans'.

Kitty sank into the feather bed and decided not to cry. She had taken a pencil and a piece of paper from the desk downstairs, and in the moonlight coming in from the window she wrote at the top: "Things I Can Do." Then she wrote, "Number 1." Kitty always felt better in a crisis if she made a list, especially if it was numbered. Under Number 1 she wrote, "Go back to the farm." That was definitely not the one she would choose. The problem, she found, was that there were no other choices. Nothing to put under Number 2 and Number 3. Kitty wanted to have at least three choices. She chewed on the lead pencil as she thought, remembering what she had read about lead poisoning. Maybe she would get poisoned and die and not have to go back to the Zachmans'. But then she would never get to go home again. She took the pencil out of her mouth.

"Number 2," she wrote. "Stay here." Aunt Katie wouldn't let her. That was hardly a choice. If only she had company at the farm. If she wasn't alone with those laughing children.

"Betsy!" she said aloud. "Betsy could go with me."

Kitty didn't feel at all sure Aunt Katie would approve of this. But it was definitely a possibility. It was definitely Number 3. "Number 3," she wrote. "Take Betsy along to the farm."

Kitty put the paper and pencil on the floor beside the bed and lay back. If she had to go back to the farm, having a friend who spoke English would help. She wouldn't be alone. It was being alone that felt so bad. Why, with Betsy there, it could be like being at the lake, like camping. They could help Aunt Katie and see the breech baby. She and Betsy could rescue Damien together. Even though Kitty hadn't seen Damien, she knew that if the Zachman children were thin, then he must be, too. He might even be starving.

The next morning Kitty put her old clothes on. She wouldn't make the mistake of dressing up to go to the farm again. When she got downstairs, Aunt Katie had just come from Mass and was stirring oatmeal on the wood stove.

"Aunt Katie, can Betsy come along to the farm with us? If I go," she added.

"Betsy? What would Betsy come along for?" said Aunt Katie.

"I want her to," said Kitty.

Aunt Katie didn't even seem interested. She

put Kitty's oatmeal on the table and poured her milk. "Sit down and eat now," she said.

"Well, can I?"

"Can you what?"

"Can I ask Betsy to come along to the farm?"

"*Ach,* no, Kitty."

"Please, Aunt Katie. I won't go back there without her," she said.

Aunt Katie looked like she was thinking. Kitty decided to cry to show that she was serious.

"All right," said Aunt Katie, foreseeing a scene like the one the night before. "You can ask her. Maybe she won't come."

Kitty finished her breakfast and cleared her dishes from the table and ran out the screen door to Betsy's house. She knocked on her back door and called her name. Betsy came to the door in her pajamas, eating a piece of toast.

"What are you doing home?" asked Betsy. "I heard Agatha had her baby. Didn't you go to the farm?"

Kitty told Betsy part of the story, leaving out the details of the farm. She hurried over the part about her running away. "Anyway," said Kitty breathlessly, "I came to ask you to come along to the farm with me today."

"To Zachmans'?" said Betsy in surprise. "Not on your life. Why would I want to go out there?"

"We could have fun," said Kitty. "And we'd get to help with the baby."

Betsy came out and sat on the back steps. Kitty sat down beside her.

"I don't think so," said Betsy.

Kitty felt desperate. She told Betsy the whole story. "Please, Betsy, won't you come along? I think Damien might be starving," she added. "It is up to us to rescue him."

Betsy thought awhile. "If you want me to come that badly, I s'pose I could ask my mother."

Kitty closed her eyes and said a Hail Mary so that Betsy's mother would say yes. There were so many hurdles to clear. She covered her ears so she couldn't hear Betsy in the kitchen asking her mother, in case she said no.

"My mom said it's okay," said Betsy, coming out again.

Kitty had her eyes closed and her ears covered.

"Kitty! I said I can come," Betsy shouted.

"How long will we be there?"

Kitty jumped up and threw her arms around Betsy. "Oh, I'm so glad! A couple of days, I guess."

"I'll pack my stuff and come over," Betsy said.

Kitty ran back to Aunt Katie's, hardly able to believe her good luck. Staying at the farm took on a whole new light. She would have an ally. "Betsy can come along," she shouted to Aunt Katie, who was emptying the dishwater at the edge of the garden.

The sun was bright and warm as Kitty and Betsy and Aunt Katie waited in the alley later that morning for Mr. Zachman and his horse. "Here he comes!" shouted Kitty, with all the exuberance she had lacked the day before. Betsy looked sleepy and not too excited. Mr.

Zachman had the same expression he always wore and didn't look surprised to see the two girls with Aunt Katie.

"Wie geht's," said Betsy as she climbed on the wagon. Kitty began to wish she knew a few German words like Betsy did.

The wagon bounced along as it had the day before. Betsy was whistling and pointing out things of interest along the way, such as the public school she went to every day. Before long the wagon turned into the littered yard that Kitty had come to dread. Betsy whistled slowly. "What a mess," she said softly to Kitty. Kitty felt better, hearing someone say that out loud. The day before it had seemed that she was the only one to notice.

Kitty saw the Zachman children in the barnyard. She hoped they would stay there.

When they got to the house, Aunt Katie went right upstairs to Mrs. Zachman and the baby and left the girls on their own. The threadbare carpet that covered the wooden boards on the floor was littered with dirt. Through the kitchen door, the girls could see a thin gray cat sitting on the table, listlessly washing its face with a damp paw.

Betsy whistled for the second time. "Everything you said was true," she said. "This place is a mess."

Kitty shuddered. Maybe it was so bad Betsy would want to go home after all. "Let's go out in the barn," she said. "We can find Damien and see if he's all right."

Betsy shook her head. Kitty was afraid she had been right. It *was* too awful for Betsy.

"Do you know what I think?" said Betsy.

Kitty shook her head. She didn't want to know.

"I think . . ." Betsy began. "I think we should clean this place up."

Kitty looked up in surprise. Whatever Kitty had expected Betsy to say, that was not it. Kitty had seen this same mess yesterday and had never thought of cleaning it.

Betsy was already down on her hands and knees. "Help me roll this rug up," she said, moving the saggy sofa from one end of it. "We'll have to take it out and shake it."

Kitty was glad she'd worn her old clothes. If Betsy wanted to clean, she was ready. The girls moved the furniture from the rug. They got warmer and warmer and dustier and dustier. By the time the rug was rolled up, Kitty was all out of breath and had to sit on the sofa and rest.

"Come on," said Betsy, who still had lots of energy. "Let's get this thing out in the yard."

The girls grunted and groaned and pulled and tugged until they had the rug out the door. Then they each took one end and shook it. Even though it was thin and threadbare, it felt very heavy.

"Now!" said Betsy when they were through. "We have to sweep that floor before we put this back. Where do you think they keep their broom?"

"I don't think they have a broom," said Kitty.

"Everyone has a broom," said Betsy, going out into the kitchen pantry. When she came out, she was rolling her eyes. "We'd better

clean in there next," she said. "And there's no broom."

"Here," called Kitty from the back porch. "Here's a broom out here."

The girls took turns sweeping the floors until all the hay and dirt was gone.

"Now," said Betsy. "We'll bring the carpet back in." The girls puffed and tugged the carpet back in. "I'll start cleaning the pantry while you unroll the rug," said Betsy.

As Kitty began to unroll the rug, the Zachman children came in the front door. They always seem to travel in a group, thought Kitty. Kitty smiled at them. She could afford to smile now that she had Betsy along. It wasn't her alone against all of them. "Hi," she said. The children smiled and clung to the wall. They slid around the doorway and out into the kitchen.

When Kitty had finished unrolling the rug, she went out to the pump in the yard to wash her face and hands. Then she lay down on the grass and rested. It was tiring, cleaning house. She wondered if her mother got this tired when she cleaned. The only thing she let Kitty help with was dusting the baseboards every Friday, and that wasn't this hard.

Won't Aunt Katie be surprised when she sees what we've done, she thought. Kitty frowned. There was the possibility Aunt Katie wouldn't notice. Even though they had swept, everything still looked shabby. Suddenly Kitty thought of a way to make Aunt Katie notice. She'd rearrange the furniture. She would move the sofa from one wall to another.

Kitty ran back in the house and pulled and tugged some more. She finally got the sofa across the room, and put an old armchair where the sofa had been. Now they would all notice that the place was cleaner because the whole room looked different. Kitty felt proud. She liked to surprise people. She skipped out into the kitchen to see what Betsy was doing. "Wait 'til you see the living room," she said.

Betsy was busy scrubbing the pantry shelves with a wet rag. Some of the Zachman children were helping her. They didn't seem to be as quiet around Betsy, and were muttering German words to each other. *"Ach,"* Betsy said to them, sounding like Aunt Katie. "Don't put that stuff back 'til I wash the shelf."

"They don't understand you," said Kitty. "They only understand German."

"They understand," said Betsy. "I showed them."

The children smiled at Kitty.

"This is Ann." Betsy pointed over her shoulder. "And this is Elizabeth and Karl and Gertrude."

The children uttered a rush of German words at Kitty.

"They want to know what your name is," said Betsy.

"How do you know that's what they said?" asked Kitty.

Betsy shrugged her shoulders. "It sounds like they want to know," she said.

"Kitty," said Kitty, pointing to herself. "My name is Kitty."

The children smiled and repeated her name.

Then they pointed to Betsy, who was up on a chair, washing the top shelves. "Betsy," they called, but it sounded more like "Budzy."

"*Ja, ja,* Budzy," called Betsy from the chair. "I'm Budzy and she's Kiddy." Betsy laughed and the children laughed.

The thin gray cat that had been on the dining-room table walked into the pantry. "*Katze!*" shouted the Zachman children.

"Cat," said Kitty. "That is a cat."

"Cot?" said the Zachman children.

Kitty shook her head. "Cat."

"They say *a* differently," said Betsy.

The Zachman children had forgotten about cleaning the pantry and were chasing the cat around the kitchen, pointing and calling, "Cot, cot, cot."

"Table," said Kitty, feeling important in her new role as teacher. She pointed to the table. The children looked at her. Then they looked at the table and touched it. "Table," said Kitty again. "This is a table." Kitty wondered why no one had taken the time to do this before, to point out these objects and say the word for the Zachman children. Why, if someone had done this before, they would have been able to stay in school.

"Table," said the Zachman children carefully. "Table," they repeated. Then they began racing around the kitchen again, shouting "table" and "cat," "table" and "cat," "table" and "cat," and pointing them out.

"Door," shouted Kitty, rapping on the back door loudly. "This is a door."

"Door," said the children. Each one of the Zachman children rapped on the door and called its name. "Door, cat, table!" they shouted.

"They learn fast," said Kitty to Betsy. "They know three words already! And I know a German word for cat, *Katze!*"

As the day wore on, Kitty learned more German words and the Zachmans learned more English ones. She found a short pencil on the kitchen floor, and on the back of a bill from the feed mill, she drew pictures of things that were

not in the kitchen and called out their names.
"Flower," said the Zachman children when she
pointed to the picture. "Tree, cow, dog."

Then Kitty drew a picture of a girl with a
dress on and long hair. "Girl," she said to the
Zachman children.

They frowned. "Kiddy," they said. "Kiddy."

"Oh, my," said Kitty. "How will I teach them
the difference between 'girl' and 'Kitty'?"

She went into the pantry and told Betsy about
her problem. "I don't think they are ready for
that yet," Betsy said.

"Maybe you're right," Kitty said. She began
to wonder if the nuns had this problem at St.
Anthony's. She had always believed the nuns
had an easy job. If this was the way it was to
be a teacher, perhaps Kitty wouldn't be a nun,
she wouldn't enter the convent. Unless, of
course, she just taught kindergarten or became
a nursing nun.

Kitty scratched out the picture of the girl.
She pointed to the other pictures. "Flower!"
called the Zachman children in chorus. "Tree,

cow, dog!" They were satisfied with these words. They could learn the difference between "girl" and "Kitty" some other time.

Betsy finished cleaning the pantry, and Kitty took the broom and swept the kitchen floor. Then they collapsed onto kitchen chairs, pleased and tired, while the Zachman children continued to run around the house banging on objects and calling out names. When they came to something they didn't know, they came running to Kitty, pointing. She would call "chair" and "rug," and they would add them to their new vocabulary and resume their chant.

Before long Aunt Katie came down the stairs to start supper. She came through the living room and into the kitchen where Kitty and Betsy were sitting. "*Ach,* can't you two girls find anything to do?" she said.

Eight

Kitty's Discovery

Aunt Katie went out the back door to the pump.

"She didn't even notice!" said Kitty. "She didn't even notice the clean living room, or the furniture I moved."

Betsy shrugged her shoulders. "It needed to be done," she said. "I like doing stuff like that."

Kitty couldn't believe that it didn't matter to Betsy that Aunt Katie didn't appreciate all the work they had done. Kitty liked people to thank her. She always thanked people who did things for her. When Auntie Jo took her swimming in the summer, Kitty always said, "Thank you for taking me, Auntie Jo," when they got home. And at Christmas when her uncle sent a present, she always wrote a thank you note before she went to bed Christmas night. It was just plain bad manners not to thank people. How could Aunt Katie have such bad manners? Maybe it wasn't manners, Kitty thought. Maybe she just didn't see what they had done. That felt even worse, somehow.

Aunt Katie came in with a pail of water and began to wash potatoes. She went into the pantry twice to get pans and didn't say anything about the clean shelves. And when the Zachman children came running up to her, hanging onto her skirt and shouting, "Table, door, cat!" she patted them on the head. *"Ja, ja,* get some plates out now."

This was the final insult. Aunt Katie didn't even notice that the Zachman children could speak English. How could she not notice that?

Kitty felt she needed fresh air. "Let's go look for Damien," she said. In all the excitement she had forgotten the thing that mattered most of all.

The girls went out the back door. On their

way to the barn Kitty shouted, "I taught them English! They can speak English and Aunt Katie never said a thing!" Betsy shrugged her shoulders.

When they got to the barn, the girls began calling for Damien. "Here, boy, here, boy," they called, looking in all the cow stalls and mangers. When he didn't come, the girls climbed up into the hayloft.

"Do you know what would be fun?" said Betsy, "If we could sleep out here tonight!"

"Really? Do you think we could really sleep out here?" asked Kitty, forgetting about Damien and the English lesson for a moment. Kitty's mind reeled at the thought. That would solve the whole awful-bedroom problem.

"Sure, we did lots of times on my uncle's farm," said Betsy. "Hey, look!" she said, leaning out of the hayloft opening. "Look who's bringing the cows home."

Kitty scrambled beside Betsy and looked out. Mr. Zachman was opening the barnyard gate, and coming along the path toward the barn was a long line of cows followed by a barking, nipping dog that was keeping them in place.

"Damien!" shouted Kitty. "Look how big he is!" Kitty couldn't believe her eyes. Instead of being skinny, Damien was twice his original size.

"I'll bet Damien gets the cows every day," said Betsy.

The girls climbed down the ladder of the hayloft and ran out to meet Damien. Kitty threw her arms around him and hugged him. "Damien," she said. "I'm so glad to see you!" She ran her hands over his soft ears and down his sleek, shiny back. Damien did not look hungry or unhappy. His tail was wagging, and he licked Kitty's face.

"He remembers you," said Betsy, patting him on his smooth black back.

"He looks happy," said Kitty. "And he isn't thin."

Mr. Zachman looked down at the girls and

smiled. Kitty was surprised to see him smile. He bent over and patted Damien on the head and said, *"Er ist ein guter Hund."*

That must mean he likes him, thought Kitty. She began to think of what a different life Damien had here from the one he would have had in St. Paul. If Kitty had won him, he would live in her mother's spotlessly clean house, in the basement at best. She thought of the small yard where he'd have to be tied to the clothesline, with no space to run. She hated to admit he was probably better off here at the farm. And he appeared to like Mr. Zachman.

Damien ran off and herded the cows into the barn, where they went into stalls to be milked. Mr. Zachman got a little three-legged stool and a pail, then sat down beside the first cow and began to milk. Every once in a while he would squirt some milk in Damien's direction, and Damien would lick it up. Yes, Damien was a good farm dog. He would not be this useful and happy in St. Paul.

Kitty sighed. She was disappointed that Damien didn't need her, and yet she was relieved that he was well and happy. She knew she couldn't take him away from the farm. But letting him go made her feel sad. It was all so confusing!

She gave Damien one last hug, and said to Betsy, "Let's ask Aunt Katie about sleeping in the hayloft!" The girls waved to Damien and Mr. Zachman and ran back to the house.

"*Ach,* sure," said Aunt Katie, waving a wooden spoon. "*Komm essen* now, *komm essen.*"

Aunt Katie had said yes. Suddenly everything about the farm felt better. The boiled potatoes in the middle of the table didn't look as bad as they had before. The Zachman children were smiling, and they looked cleaner somehow. Kitty was here on the farm with Betsy and she was going to sleep in the hayloft and she didn't have to worry about the bed with four people in it. Kitty didn't even feel angry with Aunt Katie now for not noticing all their work or the children's English words.

Mr. Zachman came in, stamping his boots. He sat down at the table and speared the potatoes with his fork. This time Kitty did the same. Everyone ate the potatoes in silence, and after the second kettle was gone, Aunt Katie got up to get a plate ready to take upstairs to Mrs. Zachman.

Betsy began to clear the plates from the table. "We can take that upstairs," she said.

Aunt Katie nodded and handed her the plate. She poured some strong black coffee into a cup and handed it to Kitty. *"Heiss,"* she said. Kitty knew that that meant "hot" and that she should be careful. Aunt Katie never wasted words.

When the girls got to the steps, Kitty felt nervous. "Betsy!" she said. "Maybe we'll see the breech baby!"

"The baby was breech?" said Betsy.

What did Betsy mean, *was?* It still is, thought Kitty. Betsy didn't seem excited about seeing it. Perhaps she has seen lots of breech babies, thought Kitty. Maybe breech was contagious and there was a lot of it around Norwood. Now Kitty wondered if it was something you could catch when you were older. Maybe it wasn't just babies that were breech—maybe she, Kitty, could be breech and start to turn purple across her face. Well, she wouldn't get too close to the baby, just in case.

The girls climbed the steps and walked down the hall. Even though it was still light outside, the hallway was dark.

"Where's her room?" asked Betsy, standing with the plate of potatoes.

"Down at the end of the hall," whispered Kitty. She didn't know why she was whispering.

When the girls came to the last door in the hallway, Betsy knocked. A voice said something in German, and the girls shoved the door open and went in. The room looked very much like the other bedroom Kitty had been in, with a metal bedstead and an old dark dresser. It was dark in the room also, but through the one window came enough light to see a woman sitting on the edge of the bed, with long hair in a braid reaching to her lap. Beside her on the bed was a knit blanket wrapped around a baby. The baby seemed to be asleep.

Betsy handed the plate to the woman, and Kitty handed her the cup of coffee. She smiled as she took them. She didn't look as frightened and tired as she had when Kitty had seen her at the church dinner. It was probably because she had had a long rest in bed, thought Kitty.

"Kitty?" she said.

"I'm Kitty," said Kitty clearly. "And this is my friend Betsy."

The woman reached out her hand to shake Betsy's. *"Danke schön, danke schön,"* she said.

"You're welcome," said Betsy.

As the woman began to eat, she said some other German words to the girls.

"We can't speak German," said Kitty.

"Can we see the baby?" said Betsy, pointing. The woman reached over and pulled the blanket away from the baby's face. Kitty closed her eyes. *"Oh,"* Kitty heard Betsy say. "Can I hold it?" Kitty cringed and shook her head. Mrs.

Zachman set her plate and cup down and lifted the baby across the bed to Betsy.

"Oh, Kitty, look how little it is!"

Kitty could feel Betsy and Mrs. Zachman looking at her. She opened her eyes. Betsy was holding the baby the way babies were supposed to be held. Kitty had never held a baby in her life.

"Look, Kitty! Look at the tiny hands!" Betsy came over to Kitty with the baby. Even though the room was dark, enough light came from the window for Kitty to see that there was no purple mark on its face. Kitty looked at the baby hard. She felt both relieved and puzzled. Was this a breech baby or wasn't it?

Betsy and Mrs. Zachman made cooing noises over the baby. They played with the little hands and patted its cheek. Kitty wasn't going to take any chances. She just stood and waited until Betsy covered the baby up and put it down on the bed beside its mother. The girls waved and said goodbye and went out the door, as Mrs. Zachman called *"Danke schön"* again.

"Betsy!" said Kitty, as soon as they were in the hall. "I thought it was a breech baby."

"Maybe it was," said Betsy.

There it was again, that word *was*. Like it was something you got over. Well, maybe it was. Maybe breech went away. Or maybe, thought Kitty, it was just hidden. Maybe the baby was purple all over its body, under the blanket, all over its legs. Kitty couldn't ask Betsy. As it was, Betsy thought city kids were dumb. She never said it, but Kitty knew she thought it.

"Breech is double," said Betsy, seeming to read Kitty's mind.

Kitty stopped stock still. Somehow it had never entered her head that breech didn't mean that awful birthmark. She must have convinced herself it did. Her mother was always talking about Kitty's wild imagination.

But *double?* Could Betsy mean twins? Surely there was only one baby. Now Kitty didn't care if Ruthie thought she was a dumb city kid. She wanted to blurt out, "What do you mean, double?" But something stopped her. She remembered what had happened at Emma's when the talk got to having babies. Everyone was uncomfortable. And Kitty remembered her father saying, "We don't talk about private things outside of the home." Well, thought Kitty, we don't talk about them at home either. She looked at Betsy who was halfway down the stairs, humming a tune. No, Betsy didn't want to talk about it either.

Kitty knew what she would do. She would put it on her list of things to find out. She took the feed bill and the little broken pencil out of her pocket and wrote, "Look up *breech* in the dictionary." She felt relieved. Kitty always felt better once something was written down. Now she could forget about it until she got home to her room in St. Paul.

Kitty and Betsy helped Aunt Katie with the dishes in the kitchen. Betsy chattered on and on about how little and cute the baby was. The Zachman children ran around the house calling out their English words. Kitty waited and waited for it to be time for bed, time to go to the hayloft.

At last Aunt Katie began to herd the children upstairs. Kitty yawned loudly, partly because she was anxious to get out to the hayloft and partly because she was really tired from all the work she and Betsy had done. "Let's get our pajamas on," she said to Betsy at last.

"Pajamas!" said Betsy. "We don't sleep in pajamas, in the hay! We sleep in our clothes."

This was a surprise to Kitty. Today had been full of surprises. To sleep in her clothes! Kitty had never done that. Even when she stayed overnight at Eileen's house, she had taken a bath and shampooed her hair and brushed her teeth and worn her pajamas and robe. She supposed tonight she wouldn't brush her teeth either. "Do we need a blanket?" she asked.

"Naw," said Betsy. "We cover up with hay."

Kitty shivered. It was surely easy to get ready for bed on a farm. It looked as if she already was.

"It would be fun to have something to eat out there, though," said Betsy.

Kitty felt relieved that some planning was necessary. "What about carrots?" she said. "I could get carrots from the garden."

"That would be good," said Betsy.

Kitty ran out the back door, glad to have a mission. She pulled some carrots from the ground and washed them at the pump. "Let's go!" she called to Betsy. "We'd better tell Aunt Katie we're going," she added, although it was more from habit than because she thought Aunt Katie would care. Aunt Katie would probably never notice the girls were gone.

Aunt Katie was pumping water to heat on the wood stove to soak clothes in overnight. When the girls told her they were going to the barn, she wiped her hands on her apron and reached up on the shelf for her worn brown purse. She opened it and took out two Hershey bars and handed one to Kitty and one to Betsy.

"For us?" said Kitty. "Are these for us?"

"*Ja,*" said Aunt Katie, setting the boilers of water on the stove.

Kitty felt she couldn't stand any more surprises in one day. She would burst. Aunt Katie never surprised people. She didn't buy Kitty presents. Her mother said it was because Aunt Katie didn't have much money. And here she was giving them candy bars. Candy bars were expensive and hard to get because of sugar rationing.

Kitty looked at Aunt Katie's hair falling in wisps around her lined face. She looked at her red, leathery hands that were always working at something, day after day. Kitty didn't love her the way she loved her mother and father, but she decided there must be other kinds of love, even for someone who rarely talked to you, because at that moment she felt herself loving Aunt Katie. She handed Betsy the carrots and went up to Aunt Katie and gave her a hug. "Thank you, Aunt Katie."

"*Ach,* go on with you," said Aunt Katie, brushing her away. All of a sudden Kitty knew that it didn't matter if Aunt Katie brushed her away or didn't notice that she had cleaned or taught the children English. Aunt Katie had her own private way of showing love.

The girls gathered their carrots and candy bars and ran out into the starry country night. They entered the dark barn and crawled up the ladder to the hayloft, where they found the softest spot for a bed and piled the hay to make a pillow. Looking out of the hayloft opening, they said, "Star light, star bright, first star I see tonight," and made wishes. They ate the carrots and candy bars and talked about their friends and school and the Zachmans. Just after they finished telling ghost stories, they heard a noise.

"Someone's coming up here!" whispered Kitty.

They listened, motionless. The girls heard footsteps in the hay. Then Kitty felt a wet nose nudge her leg.

"Damien!" she said. "Betsy, it's Damien! He came to spend the night with us!"

Kitty threw her arms around the dog's neck, and he lay down in the hay between her and Betsy and went to sleep. Betsy finished the last of her Hershey bar and said good night. Then she, too, turned over in the hay and fell asleep.

Kitty lay for a long while looking out at the stars and enjoying the sweet smell of the hay. She felt that she must smell it very deeply and look very long and hard at the stars to try and hold onto this moment. She had never had one like it, and she knew it would never come again. On Saturday she would be going home to St. Paul, where things like this didn't happen.

In her mind, Kitty made a list of all the things she'd accomplished this summer and the things she hadn't. She lined them up. She had found out that breech babies didn't have marks on their faces. She *hadn't* found out what they were . . . yet. She had bought a pagan baby of her very own. She *hadn't* won a dog. She had gone back to the farm. She had taught the Zachman children some English words. She had discovered that Aunt Katie loved her. Suddenly there seemed to be more "hads" than "hadn'ts." Kitty turned over in the hay, and fell asleep.